WHAT Others Are Saying

Old Acquaintances pulls the reader into an intriguing world of mystery, romance and suspense that will send chills down your spine! Survival is the goal and emotions rule the day as the face of darkness and the reality of fear draw the reader into a suspense filled escape. A quick, enjoyable and thrilling mystery-romance novel that speaks to the heart; I urge everyone to take this book home and then, prepare for the adventure!

—S. B. Newman
Author of, *The Night Eagles Soared*

Old Acquaintances...grabbed my attention from the first page and didn't let go until the last page. With twists and turns, thrills and chills, and just the right amount of romance...Old Acquaintances is the perfect escape from reality."

—C. Swinney
Financial Services Accounting Manager for a leading home care agency...and avid book reader

OLD ACQUAINTANCES

ursula gorman

OLD ACQUAINTANCES

[a novel]

TATE PUBLISHING & *Enterprises*

Old Acquaintances
Copyright © 2010 by Ursula Gorman. All rights reserved.

No part of this publication may be reproduced, stored in a retrieval system or transmitted in any way by any means, electronic, mechanical, photocopy, recording or otherwise without the prior permission of the author except as provided by USA copyright law.

This novel is a work of fiction. Names, descriptions, entities, and incidents included in the story are products of the author's imagination. Any resemblance to actual persons, events, and entities is entirely coincidental.

The opinions expressed by the author are not necessarily those of Tate Publishing, LLC.

Published by Tate Publishing & Enterprises, LLC
127 E. Trade Center Terrace | Mustang, Oklahoma 73064 USA
1.888.361.9473 | www.tatepublishing.com

Tate Publishing is committed to excellence in the publishing industry. The company reflects the philosophy established by the founders, based on Psalm 68:11,
"The Lord gave the word and great was the company of those who published it."

Book design copyright © 2010 by Tate Publishing, LLC. All rights reserved.
Cover design by Lauran Levy
Interior design by Jeff Fisher
Author photo courtesy of Suzanne Jordan Hill

Published in the United States of America

ISBN: 978-1-61739-099-9
1. Fiction, Romance, Suspense
2. Fiction, Mystery & Detective, General
10.08.30

ACKNOWLEDGMENTS

THERE ARE A NUMBER OF people I need to thank. First, my husband, Tim; he has encouraged me to follow my dreams from the moment we meet almost eighteen years ago. Without his encouragement, I might never have taken on this endeavor. To my daughter and son, Beth and Shane, for their love and for reminding me what fun imagination can be. I pray that they never lose theirs. To my parents, Keith and Ruth, and my sister, Leatha, who have encouraged me from the beginning. To Aunt Juanita, Aunt Peggy, and Uncle Frank for their love and support. Though they are miles away, they are always in my heart. To the ladies at work for their encouragement, especially to Kristin, my sounding board, and Carmen, for being a fresh pair of eyes. To J. Davis and the Brazells for their support of a stranger; I believe there is no kinder act than the kindness shown to a stranger. To my brother, Alan, I hope to be reading your book someday. To my sister-in-law, Suzanne, for letting me bounce ideas off you. Thank you all for your love, support, and encouragement. This book is for all of you with love!

Above all else, I give the glory to God. With his love and strength all things are possible.

CHAPTER 1

ONCE AGAIN, RISSA NEIL WAS the only one left to lock up. It was of her own doing. Her small boutique—her dream since she'd been little—had been showing a steady incline thanks to the extra hours she'd put into it since her mom's death two years earlier. Her personal life, on the other hand, had shown a steady decline for the same reason. She really didn't miss dating, but she'd neglected friendships, and it showed. Only one true friend had stuck by her since her mom's death.

Matt Johns understood, having lost his parents in a skiing accident when he was eighteen. He'd had trouble adjusting with being an adult orphan. His parents had been rich, and a lot of people came out of the woodwork to offer him help and guidance. That is, until they found out that he couldn't touch the money until he graduated college or turned twenty-five, whichever came first.

Rissa and her mom had taken Matt under their wings during that difficult first year of his parents' accident. They asked for nothing; they only wanted to be there for him. During that year he was at their house a lot for support, advice, home-cooked meals, and things he missed being able to do with his parents. He and Rissa had become very close during that time, a bond that went beyond friendship and became the one relationship they both treasured beyond any other.

Rissa stopped walking when she heard a noise. It was late, and the parking lot was dark. The only light was from a meager streetlight too far away to be of any help. Rissa stood still, listening to the night. She wasn't sure what had caught her attention, only that there had been a noise that didn't belong.

Rissa started walking, wishing she'd parked closer to the store. There it was again. She started walking faster while trying to find her keys, realizing how vulnerable she was. This was a shopping district, and no one was out at this time of night.

She thought she heard footsteps coming from the bushes that edged the parking lot. She took off running to her car as a dark figure stepped out of the bushes. In her haste to unlock her car door, she dropped her purse. She carried one of those big purses men always teased women about, and for good reason—she carried everything but the kitchen sink in it. The contents of her purse scattered all over the pavement and under her car. She tried to grab as much as she could while constantly looking over her shoulder toward the area she thought the noise had come from. Leaving her keys hanging in the lock, she used both hands to frantically shove her brush and her wallet, along with her makeup bag and the novel she had been reading, back into her bag. She wasn't concerned about some of the smaller stuff she saw laying around. The parking lot was so dark she wasn't sure she would be able to find it all anyway. She was more worried about whatever had made the sounds she heard. Figuring she was pressing her luck, she left everything else on the ground, got in her car, and locked the door.

As she pulled out of the lot, she made sure her headlights shone on the area where she had seen the shadow—nothing. "Stupid imagination," Rissa said with a forced laugh, but she knew she hadn't imagined it.

As she pulled out, a shadow emerged from the bushes, walked to where Rissa had been parked, and picked something up that had fallen underneath the car.

"MATT, I'M FINE. I TOLD you, it was my imagination." Rissa regretted the impulse to call Matt. She had been trying to convince him she was okay when she wasn't even convinced herself.

"Rissa, honey, you don't get worked up over nothing. When are you going to start leaving at a decent time?" This was Matt's favorite topic; he was trying to get her back into the world again. It seemed to be working, since she'd agreed to go to a concert with him. Granted, it wasn't anything crazy, but even the college symphony was better than nothing.

Rissa knew that the symphony wasn't going to find her too many dates, but they weren't going strictly for her; it was for Laura. Laura was Matt's girlfriend of just over a year, and that was a record since Matt's girlfriends didn't usually last very long.

Laura was the assistant conductor of the Jameson College Symphony. While being conductor held great respect and honor; being assistant didn't.

"I can come over," Matt said.

"I'm okay, really."

Matt sighed, making Rissa smile. "Fine, have it your way."

"Good night, Matt. Love you."

"Love you too, brat!"

THE MORNING SUN ON RISSA'S face was an unwelcome reminder that she forgot to pull the blinds when she went to bed. In the daylight, last night's scare seemed surreal. Rissa could almost forget it happened—almost. As was her morning routine, she started the coffee maker then went to take her shower. By the time she added conditioner to her hair she'd almost convinced herself that last night hadn't happened.

"Why would anyone stand in the dark and watch me? I saw them; they had to know that." Rissa let out a frustrated growl. "It had to be a homeless person. I probably scared him as much as he scared me."

Rissa was still going over last night's events when she walked into the kitchen ten minutes later, her hair wrapped in a towel and a big fluffy robe on to help ward off the chill of a late September morning. As she was taking her first sip of coffee the phone rang, making her jump, sloshing coffee over her hand. "Ahhh!" Rissa yelled, sticking her hand under cold water. Keeping her hand under the water, she reached over with her other hand and grabbed the phone.

"Hello," she growled into the phone.

"Good morning, sunshine," Matt chirped. "I was calling to see how you are doing. Did the demons leave with the night?"

"Yeah, sorry, the phone startled me and I spilled my coffee. I'm feeling better this morning."

Matt laughed. "Sounds like it!" Changing subjects, Matt said, "I've got an errand to run; want to go?"

"Where? Are you cancelling tonight?" She almost wished he were. She needed more sleep and hoped to go to bed early.

"I have to go check on the country house. There was a report of a possible break in. I don't think it's anything, but I have to be sure. And no, I'm not cancelling tonight. We should be back no later than two."

When Matt's parents died, everything went to Matt, and that included their house in the country. It was huge and sat on eighteen acres with a driveway that looked two miles long. You could see anyone coming long before they ever got there. Matt rarely went out there, but he couldn't bring himself to sell it.

"Want to go? The fresh air might do you good."

"Sounds good. A relaxing car ride is just what I need," answered Rissa.

"Great, be there in thirty minutes; don't keep me waiting." Matt hung up before Rissa could reply.

"Big buffoon," she muttered affectionately.

Matt was right; the ride to and from the country house was relaxing. The crisp fall air blowing in the open windows felt wonderful. Rissa had worn a lightweight sweater in anticipation of a long country drive with the windows down, and she was glad she had. It wouldn't be long until the leaves fell from the trees, but for now they were a beautiful cacophony of riotous colors. The leaves had turned colors earlier this season due to lower than normal temperatures, but Rissa loved this time of year and welcomed the change. While the drive was unnecessary since apparently there was no break-in, Rissa was glad for the relaxing drive.

"The country air agrees with you."

"What do you mean?"

"You have color in your cheeks and you're relaxed. When I picked you up this morning you were pale and tense. You didn't sleep well, did you?"

"No, I guess I didn't. Too much adrenaline. But I do feel much better."

"The concert won't get over until pretty late; why don't you come home with me afterward? You can get a good night's sleep."

"Why, Matt, are you making a pass at me?" Rissa said, with a shocked expression.

"Oh, shut up!" Matt spat out.

After a beat of silence they both started laughing. "Oh, Matt, I do love you! I promise I'm all right. I have to work in the morning, and as soon as you drop me off tonight, I'm hitting the hay. Saturdays are busy days, and I can't be late since Tina won't be in."

"Let me know if you change your mind." Matt looked at Rissa. "By the way, I love you too!"

THE NEXT MORNING RISSA WAS up early, this time because of work. She'd promised Tina, her assistant, that she could have the day off for her one-year anniversary with her boyfriend. Tina wanted to look extra special for the day, so Rissa sent her to her hair stylist at A Cut Above and Mindi had worked her magic.

Rissa didn't mind filling in for Tina, but she needed time away from the store; she needed balance back in her life. Seeing Matt and Laura together last night at the concert made her realize that life went on with or without her, and she decided she didn't want to be left behind.

Arriving at work, Rissa pulled into her usual spot then, reconsidering, moved the car closer to the entrance. "I need to make sure I get out on time," Rissa muttered.

The day flew by, and Rissa was able to leave while there were still plenty of people milling around. There was a café a couple doors down that didn't close until ten. Rissa made a mental note to leave by ten every night. Getting in her car, she noticed something on her windshield. She reached over and picked up a single rose. "Matt, have you been worrying?" Rissa said aloud when she didn't find a card. Smiling, she got in and drove down the road, but her smile vanished as she heard the announcement on the radio:

"Early this morning, police responded to a nine-one-one call at the Abner estate. Teresa Abner, daughter of Mitchell Abner, was found dead this morning. The cause of death has yet to be released, but it is being treated as a homicide. Police are looking at Teresa Abner's ex-husband, Lester Wilkes, as a person of interest. But at this time they are not ruling out a revenge killing by someone Mitchell Abner helped convict. As you know, Mitchell Abner, is the prominent attorney—" Rissa tuned out the news broadcast.

"Oh my…" Rissa's cell started ringing. "Hello."

"Hey, hear the news about Teresa?" Matt asked.

"Yeah, can you believe it?"

"I'm shocked. With all the death threats her dad's been getting, you'd think they'd have better security."

"I haven't seen Teresa in years. She has a little boy; he should be about six now."

"I thought she was married; did she keep her maiden name? Where's the husband?"

"He's been gone since before the baby was born. He was a deadbeat musician. I heard him play once. I had a headache for two days. He told Teresa that with all the money her dad was worth he shouldn't have to work." Rissa continued, "Anyway, when Teresa found out she was pregnant he didn't stick around. He left, she filed for divorce, he signed, and they went their separate ways."

"Man, he sucks! Do you think he did it?"

"After six years, why would he come back and kill her?"

"The boy? Maybe he changed his mind, wanted to see his boy, and she refused."

"Doesn't hold. He signed away all parental rights. He never even knew if it was a boy or girl."

"A lot could have changed over the years," Matt said, playing devil's advocate.

"I guess you are right. Still…"

THE DAYS WENT BY WITHOUT incident, and Rissa forgot all about the strange scare she had had. The news kept bringing up the Abner story; after all, Mitchell Abner was a well-known attorney.

A week after the murder, with no new leads, the police were forced to release details about how Teresa was killed. It wasn't pretty; she had been stabbed repeatedly. According to police, the killer came in her bedroom window and left the same way, never venturing out into the rest of the house even though everyone was asleep and would have been easy victims. The police figured it was a message for Mr. Abner since Teresa's ex had been located in California, still trying to get his big break, and had an airtight alibi. He had been in jail at the time of the murder for public intoxication and indecent exposure. Rissa sat down to watch the ten o'clock news to see if there was an update. There wasn't, but there was something else.

"Tonight, a fatal carjacking in the city. Twenty-three-year-old Mindi Andrews was the victim of an apparent attempted carjacking outside trendy salon, A Cut Above. Miss Andrews was reportedly leaving her place of employment, and it's assumed she tried to fight off the carjacker, which led to her being stabbed multiple times. The carjacker was scared off by people in the area responding to Miss Andrews' screams. Miss Andrews died en route to the hospital."

Rissa was in shock. "What a week; first I get frightened leaving work, then Teresa is killed, and now Mindi is killed!" Rissa felt as if she had been dealt a blow to the stomach. She was having trouble breathing and the room felt as if it were spinning. "Mindi…" Rissa moaned. While they hadn't been social friends, they had become close during their talks while Mindi did Rissa's hair. Mindi was on cloud nine the last time Rissa had seen her. She had just become engaged and was hoping to be able to save up enough money to open her own salon. She had been so young and had so much living to do.

Rissa reached over to call Matt then stopped, remembering the call she had made after her parking lot scare. She didn't think she could handle dealing with Matt's concern tonight, so she took a sleeping pill instead and went to bed.

RISSA TRIED TO LISTEN FOR any updates on Teresa and Mindi's cases since hearing about Mindi's attack on Saturday night. She hadn't had a chance to catch any news updates during the day on the Wednesday after Mindi's attack, due to a busy day at the store. So the first thing she did when she got home from work was check the news. The most recent reports kept playing the same stories about the cases having no further leads, but Rissa couldn't seem to pull herself away from any and all news on her friends. Tonight there was a new story, but it wasn't about Teresa or Mindi. At first Rissa didn't pay too close attention since she didn't know the people involved, but something about the scene caught her attention. It had just been a quick image that had flashed on the screen, and Rissa couldn't put her finger on exactly what had caught her attention. She listened to the rest of the news story, hoping that whatever it had been would come back on.

"Late last night the police received a frantic nine-one-one call from a fifteen-year-old male. He stated that his parents, Nick and Serena Young, had been hurt. The police arrived at the scene to discover a double homicide. Details are sketchy, but it appears that the teen had gone to watch a local college game with a schoolmate and his parents; they dropped him off at home approximately ten thirty last night. The nine-one-one call came in ten minutes later. What the boy saw isn't clear, and the police aren't releasing much information at this time, except to say that it is being treated as a homicide and that the boy is not a suspect."

The camera pulled back from the newscaster to include the house with police tape on it. Rissa knew that house; she knew that house very well. That's what had caught her eye. The newscaster was standing in front of the house, and she had recognized it during the brief glimpse she had gotten. Steve and Ariel Bennington, friends of her mom, had once lived there.

"What's going on? This is crazy!" Rissa got up and paced back and forth in her living room. Granted, the Benningtons didn't still live there, but it was still too close for comfort.

"MAN, YOU LOOK BAD. ARE you okay?" Tina asked when Rissa walked in to work Thursday morning.

"No, I'm beat. I had a rough night." The Benningtons were safe and it wasn't anyone she knew...so why was it affecting her the way it was? She hadn't slept at all, and it wasn't a great ending to her week. Rissa always enjoyed the end of the week at work because it was her busiest time, but not today. She just wanted the day to be over so she could go back home and crawl into bed.

"Look, everything's under control; why don't you take the day off? Actually, now that you've hired a couple of part-timers, take a couple days off."

"You don't mind?" Normally Rissa would never have agreed to take an unplanned weekend off, especially a four-day weekend, but she wasn't about to look this gift horse in the mouth.

"Of course not. It's time you took a little time for yourself. The store's going strong, and we're fully staffed."

Without giving Tina a chance to rescind the offer, Rissa jumped at the opportunity. "Thanks, Tina. I owe you. I'll be back on Monday, but if anything comes up, give me a call."

"Don't worry; go have fun."

Rissa said good-bye and headed home to pack. It'd been so long since she had played hooky that she couldn't think of a single place to go. She sat on her bed with a solid thump. "Oh, Mom, how have I let my life come to this? I have an extended weekend and can afford to do whatever I want, and I can't think of a single thing." The realization of how detached she'd become hit her with the force of a freight train. She felt ashamed. She knew her mom would have been disappointed at the current status of her life, but that was going to change starting now.

With that, Rissa decided to go to a spa a couple hours out of town. She made a quick call to make sure they could take her for some treatments and booked the deluxe spa package. Feeling better, she grabbed her suitcase and headed for the door.

Rissa was momentarily startled when she opened the door to find Matt standing there with his fist raised to knock. "What are you doing here?" she asked as she quickly regained her composure.

"Well, good morning to you too, sweetheart!"

"Sorry, I wasn't expecting you."

"Obviously. I went by the store, and Tina told me

you were taking some time off." After a slight pause Matt added, "So what's the matter?"

"I don't know why I try. You always know when something's bothering me."

"Honey, we've known each other too long and been through too much. You always know when things aren't right with me too. Now, tell me what's bothering you."

"It's stupid," Rissa said as she stepped back in a silent invitation for Matt to come in.

"You've never been stupid. Talk," Matt demanded as he walked into the living room.

"Okay. Don't make fun of me though." Rissa took a deep breath and started talking on her exhale, "You remember the other night when I called and said someone was watching me?" Rissa didn't wait for a reply. "Well, several things have happened since then. Soon after that, two people I know were killed."

"Two? I know about Teresa, but who else?"

Rissa knew she should have told Matt about Mindi right away, but at first she had been overcome with shock and couldn't handle another episode of Matt trying to get her to come stay with him. She loved Matt, but since her mother's death he had become overprotective. She knew he only had her best interest at heart, but the longer she waited to tell Matt about Mindi, the harder it had become to bring the subject up. Rissa decided to just come out with it and beg for his forgiveness for hurting his feelings. "Mindi Andrews was killed a couple of days after Teresa."

"I heard about that." Matt had an odd look on his face. "How do you know her?" Before Rissa could answer Matt continued. "Oh wait, I knew her name sounded familiar, but I couldn't place it. She was the woman you went to, to have your hair done. Why are you just now telling me about it?"

"I'm sorry, Matt. I was worried you would think I was overreacting, and I didn't want you worrying about me."

Matt still had the odd look on his face and paused as though he was going to say one thing and changed his mind and said, "Nothing is going to stop me from worrying about you, Rissa. It's just part of the deal. And it's just a coincidence that you knew both of them. I've been following the Abner case in the news, so of course I've heard about Mindi since her case has been all over the news too, but I haven't heard anything about them being related."

"No, they aren't. At least, I don't think so." Rissa paused, and Matt knew there was more. "About a week after Mindi was killed, I heard about a couple that was killed in their home."

"You knew them too?" Matt looked skeptical.

"No. But I knew the people who used to live there. I've been to that house many times."

"Okay, I admit it's a huge coincidence, but that's all it is."

She paced back and forth. How could she explain a feeling? How could she know two people who had been murdered and have a connection to a double murder, albeit a thin connection?

"Look, honey, maybe you do need to get away for a bit. How about the two of us go to the mountains? We could get a little skiing in over the weekend. Laura is on the road with the symphony, and I don't have any pressing plans that can't be changed. I can call Laura and let her know what's going on and where she can reach me; she will understand."

And she would. Matt had had some bad relationships in the past, mainly due to their friendship, but Laura was different than the other women Matt had dated. The other women hadn't understood their relationship. They always gave him the ultimatum of them or her, usually without her even knowing about it until after he'd quit seeing them. Matt told Laura up front about their relationship, that it was completely platonic. He also let her know anyone who didn't accept her needn't get involved with him. Laughing, Laura said it showed he knew how to respect women if they'd remained such good friends over the years. She welcomed Rissa with open arms, as Rissa had done with her.

"I appreciate it, but I've already made plans, and other than you and Tina, I would prefer no one know where I'm at. I need a little time to myself, and the fewer people that know where I am, the better." Rissa hugged Matt. "I'll have my cell in case either of you need me."

Matt carried her suitcase to the car. "Oh, I've been meaning to say thanks for the rose you left on my car after my scare in the parking lot. With everything that has been going on I forgot to thank you."

Matt looked confused; then a sparkle lit his eyes. "You know roses aren't my style. I think someone's got an admirer."

While Rissa seriously doubted that, she didn't say anything and pushed the thought of the rose out of her mind.

RISSA FELT BAD ABOUT NOT going skiing with Matt, but she needed to be alone. She couldn't help but be disturbed by her old acquaintances' deaths. She hadn't seen Teresa in years, and she only knew Mindi from the salon, but she couldn't quit thinking about them.

By Saturday Rissa was feeling better than she had in a long time. She was enjoying an hour-long massage when her cell phone rang. The masseuse didn't look pleased but knew that the clients paid enough money to be interrupted if they chose to be. Rissa didn't want to be interrupted, but she knew it would be either Matt or Tina, so she answered it.

"Hello?"

"Hi, darling. How is the rehab center?" Matt's warped sense of humor never failed to make Rissa smile.

"Funny! Did you just call to be cute?"

"You think I'm cute? I'm flattered," Matt joked. "I wanted to see how you were doing; I miss you. You sounded like you were asleep. Am I bothering you?"

"No, I wasn't asleep, and yes, you are bothering me," Rissa teased Matt. "I'm having a massage, and you're ruining the ambiance."

"Wow! The girl knows how to put me in my place."

Rissa smiled. "As if you'd let anyone put you in your place." She heard Matt make a sound she took as agreement. Matt was nothing if not confident. He had never been lacking in that area. Rissa had always been glad that she could be herself around him without fear of offending him. Rissa wasn't mean, but her humor was often mistaken for meanness instead of the good-natured orneriness it was.

"When're you coming home? I miss you terribly. You're ruining my relationship with Laura!"

Rissa sat up abruptly, almost losing her towel. The masseuse made a disgusted sound and left the room. "Has she given you the ultimatum? I didn't think she'd do that. You love each other. Why'd she wait until I was gone? I can't believe this. How dare she? I'm coming back and kicking her butt!"

"*Rissa!*" Matt yelled.

"What?" Rissa was breathing hard.

"I started out enjoying your tirade, but I'm afraid you really will come back and kick her butt," Matt said with a chuckle.

"What's so funny? What's going on?"

"I meant that I bug her so much that she's threatening to break things off if you don't come back and take up some of my time. She got back earlier than expected and has been trying to pry your secret location out of me so she can go get you and drag you back home. Since I won't tell her where you are, I had to give her something, so I told her when you planned on coming home. She's been counting the hours until you come home."

"Sorry about jumping to conclusions." After a slight pause Rissa added, "You could have told her where I'm at. I don't want to cause any problems between you two, and keeping secrets isn't ever good in a relationship."

"Aw, she wasn't really mad that I wouldn't tell her, but she's serious about needing you to take up some of my time. I guess I'm being a nuisance. And, honey, you can come to my defense anytime. I think it's adorable!"

"Kiss my butt, birdbrain!"

Matt let out a howl of laughter at the childhood expression. "Is that a come on? I thought we were beyond that!"

"I'm hanging up now!"

"Love you, Rissa," Matt said as he hung up the phone.

Rissa sat there in nothing but a towel, smiling. "Love you too, Matt."

"HOW WERE THINGS WHILE I was gone?" Rissa asked Tina. "I missed seeing everyone."

"Good, but that reminds me. Some guy kept calling for you. He wasn't happy I wouldn't tell him where you were. It was kind of creepy."

"What was his name?" asked Rissa.

"He wouldn't say. He would get mad, demand to know where you were and when you would be back, and then hang up. I'm telling you, he was weird!"

Rissa wondered who would call and not be willing to give their name. She hadn't received any unusual calls since her return Saturday night, and she didn't have any messages on her answering machine at home.

"Hey, stranger!" Matt's greeting interrupted her thoughts.

"Where've you been? After we talked Saturday, I decided to come home a day early to see you. I tried to call you, but you never answered your cell, so I expected you to be here first thing."

"Sorry, darlin', had to check out another false alarm at the country house."

"What happened?"

"Nothing."

After a slight pause Rissa said, "There's more, you look like you have something else to say. Plus, I called your cell and you always have it with you. So what gives?" Matt was turning an interesting shade of red. Rissa had never seen him blush. "Okay, give it up. What's going on?"

"Laura went with me, and we...uh...well, that is—"

"What?" Rissa was enjoying his discomfort.

"We are thinking about making that our full-time home." Matt watched as dawning came to Rissa's face.

"You're going to live together?" Rissa was astounded. She knew they were serious, but she didn't realize they were *that* serious.

"Well, yeah, after the wedding anyway."

"*What?* You're getting married?" Rissa couldn't believe it.

"That's great!" Tina said, giving Matt a hug.

"One thing led to another, and I proposed. She cried forever, and I thought she was going to say no. I didn't realize they were happy tears; I don't know if I'll ever understand women," Matt said, smiling ear to ear. "She finally said yes."

As Tina left to help a customer Matt said, "She asked me if I thought you'd be her maid of honor." Rissa gasped. "I told her no."

"Shouldn't I make that decision?" Rissa asked.

"I told her you were already busy."

"How could you possibly know that?"

"I was hoping you'd be my best man—or best friend or best woman—whatever you want to call it." He was fumbling with his words but could tell by her watery smile that it didn't matter.

She threw her arms around his neck. "Matt, I'd be honored." Pulling back from the hug, Rissa looked up at Matt. "Is it okay with Laura? I mean, does she have a problem with a female best man?"

"She loved the idea. She laughed and said it was perfect. Said she'd ask her roommate to be her maid of honor. She doesn't have many close friends, and her mom's her only family, and they aren't close. She doesn't even want her at the wedding."

"That's sad. It's terrible to have family and not have anything to do with them. All I had was my mom, and I would give anything to have her back. All Laura has is her mom, and she has cut her off. Maybe time will heal whatever happened between them. I know how important family is, and I hate that she has cut off the only person she has."

"I know, but she's insistent. She had a bad childhood and won't talk about it. She won't even tell me anything about her mom. She won't talk about her past or even tell me a single thing about her childhood. What can I do?"

They were both silent, lost in their own thoughts.

Trying to shake the melancholy mood, she looked up at Matt and asked, "When do we celebrate?"

WITH MATT, WHEN YOU ASK a question, be prepared for the answer. Rissa had such a headache the next morning from "celebrating" that six aspirin had barely touched the pain.

The ringing of the phone had her cussing and covering her ears. She knew it wasn't Matt. He drank more than she did, plus, he knew not to call after the kind of night they had. Rissa didn't know of anyone else who would need her bad enough that they couldn't wait until after her shower. She kept walking and heard the machine pick up.

She stood under the spray until the water started to cool. She hurriedly washed her hair before the water became too cold to bear. She heard the phone ringing again as she stepped out of the shower. She let the machine get it again.

Walking to the kitchen to get a much-needed cup of coffee, she noticed the answering machine was showing four missed calls. She started to worry that something was wrong with Matt. She'd only heard the phone ring twice, so it must have rang two times while she was in the shower. She hit the message button. The first three were hang ups. The fourth call made chills go up her spine.

"I know you're there; why aren't you answering? You can't hide from me. I'm watching you. I know you're home. I watched the cab drop you off early this morning, and you haven't left. Are you still asleep? That was some night you had. It's not good to drink that much. Come on; I know you're there. *Pick up the phone!*" A low, guttural voice spit the venomous words through the answering machine.

Rissa didn't realize she was backing up until she hit the wall. Startled, she spun around shaking, scared by the voice on the phone. She went back to the phone and called Matt.

"This had better be important!" Matt growled.

"Matt," Rissa cried.

"Rissa, what's wrong?" Matt instantly became alert at Rissa's cry.

"Matt, I'm scared. Someone's been watching me."

"I'm on my way!" With that he hung up, and Rissa waited.

CHAPTER 2

RISSA AND MATT PLAYED THE message again, only this time they weren't alone. After Matt heard it for the first time, he called the police. Rissa didn't say anything; she wasn't above asking for help. She was scared spitless!

The first officer introduced himself as Detective Wright. He was overweight and smelled slightly of sweat. His clothing was neat but a little too tight around the midsection, and he wore his tie slightly askew. His palms were clammy when Rissa shook his hand, but Rissa liked him right away. He was intelligent, she could tell by the questions he asked and the way he seemed to absorb everything around him. He looked at Rissa with sympathy and spoke with understanding. Rissa knew instinctively that if they played good cop/bad cop, Detective Wright would play the good cop.

That brought her to his partner—a completely different story. He'd introduced himself as Detective

Stone. He was tall, had jet black hair, and his eyes were so dark she couldn't tell what color they were. He had a ruggedness about him that Rissa found attractive; no, if she were being honest with herself she would have to admit he was sexy. He was dressed similarly to his partner, in slacks and a dress shirt, but without the tie. But that's where the similarities ended. Detective Stone wore his clothes as if they were tailor made for him. You could tell he was muscular, even though it wasn't because he was trying to announce the fact; the shirt just fit him that well. Rissa had a hard time looking away, and she realized she was staring when she caught his quizzical look. She felt herself blush and quickly looked away.

"Does the voice sound familiar, Ms. Neil?"

"No, and as hateful as it is, I think I would remember it," Rissa said, shuddering.

"Have you had a bad breakup recently?" Detective Wright asked.

"No, I haven't dated in a while," Rissa said uncomfortably.

"I find that hard to believe, Ms. Neil," Detective Wright said.

Rissa looked up at him and then over to Detective Stone. Detective Stone hadn't said anything since the introductions were made, but the way he watched her was unnerving. He had a stillness about him that made you realize he was taking in every word, every detail. Even as he stayed on the edges of the conversation, you felt as if he were the one in control of the meeting. And though the man had hardly said a word, he was the dominant presence in the room.

"Her mother died two years ago, and she hasn't really gotten back out there. She's buried herself in her work," Matt answered, helping her to break eye contact with the sexy detective.

"Two years?" Detective Stone sounded skeptical and had Rissa swinging her gaze back to him.

"I'm sorry, Detective; I didn't realize that it would offend you for a single woman not to date." Rissa wasn't sure why the detective's comment bothered her, but she had bristled immediately and went on the defensive.

Detective Stone held his hands up in mock surrender but didn't bother to hide his smile. "Ms. Neil, it doesn't offend me. I'm just surprised a woman of your unquestionable good looks hasn't dated in two years." Rissa just stared at him. "Mr. Johns, if you're not her boyfriend, what's your connection in all of this?"

"We're friends," Rissa answered for him. "When I heard the message I called Matt right away. He came over, listened to it, and immediately called you." Rissa didn't like Matt being questioned; her hands were clenched in fists.

"I didn't mean to imply that he was involved in threatening you, Ms. Neil. I need to get all the facts straight before I move forward in the investigation,"

Detective Stone said. "There's no need to get defensive. We're here to help you, remember?"

"I know that. What makes you think I'm getting defensive?" Rissa turned red when Detective Stone pointedly looked down at her closed fists. She made herself relax her hands and took a deep breath, then another one. "I'm sorry. I guess the message upset me more than I realized, and on top of last night…" She trailed off.

"What about last night?" Detective Wright asked, alert.

"Oh, nothing happened, sorry to give that impression. We went out last night to celebrate Matt's engagement, and we both drank too much!"

Detective Wright looked at Matt. "Congratulations!"

"Thanks," Matt said with a lopsided grin. Seeing the exchange had Rissa smiling too, until she looked over and saw Detective Stone watching her. He had very intense eyes, and she found herself having a hard time breaking eye contact again. He gave her a smile that said he knew what she was thinking. She stopped smiling and looked away. *He can't possibly know what I'm thinking,* she told herself. She glanced up again, but he was writing something in his notebook; there was a small smile on his lips. She could feel her pulse beating rapidly and felt flustered when Stone looked back up and caught her watching him.

"Anything else happen lately?" Detective Stone asked. He was fascinated by her reaction to him;

she seemed nervous and wary but also curious. She blushed a lot, but only when she spoke to him or when he caught her watching him. He found it hard to believe she hadn't dated in two years. She had a very nice figure with curves where they looked best on a woman. Her mouth drew his attention. She had the kind of lips you wanted to kiss to see if they were as soft as they looked. And even though he knew the threatening message had upset her, she was poised and composed. He also knew that she was loyal to her friends and that could sometimes be a mistake. When you have been threatened the way she has, you tend to overlook those closest to you.

"What about that night about a month ago when you thought someone was watching you?" Matt asked.

"When was that?" Detective Wright asked.

"Matt's right; it's been about three or four weeks. I left work one night and thought I heard some noises. I panicked and took off running to my car, spilling my purse in the process. I thought I saw a figure step out of the hedges, but once I got in my car and turned on the headlights, there was no one there."

"Anything else?" Detective Stone asked.

"Not unless you count people I know being killed."

Rissa didn't realize she'd said that out loud until Detective Stone asked, "What are you talking about? Who's been killed?" *Unbelievable; here we are talking about a possible stalker and a threatening message, and she's connected with people being killed.*

Rissa looked at him, berating herself for having said anything. So she knew a couple of people who had died. It wasn't as if she had been in contact with them recently. "It's nothing, really. Some people I know have had horrible things happen to them recently."

"Such as?" Detective Stone asked irritably. Rissa didn't notice his attitude, but Matt and Detective Wright did. Matt knew that Detective Stone wasn't someone he would want to cross.

"Well, an old friend of mine, Teresa Abner, was killed in her home. Then another acquaintance of mine, Mindi Andrews, was killed in a carjacking." Rissa paused, unsure if she should even mention the house where the couple had been killed. After all, she didn't know them. She looked at Matt, and he gave her an encouraging nod. He might have thought she was overreacting before, but now he wasn't so sure. Taking a deep breath, she continued, "Then a teen found his parents dead when he came home from a game; while I didn't know them, I knew the couple that used to live in the house." Rissa felt stupid for saying anything and missed the look that passed between the two detectives; a lot was said in that one look. She couldn't know that all three crimes were linked. The MO was the same, but that information had been kept out of the press.

"You know, Tina said that while I was gone for the weekend someone kept calling for me," Rissa said absently.

"Who's Tina?" Detective Wright asked.

"Tina Franklin, she's my assistant at work. She covered for me while I took some time off." Rissa related what Tina had told her.

Half an hour later the detectives left, promising to be in touch. As Rissa shut the door she felt relieved and oddly disappointed that Detective Stone was gone.

DRIVING BACK TO THE PRECINCT, the detectives were each lost in their own thoughts. The killings were undoubtedly linked, and somehow Ms. Neil was involved. No other person outside the force had put the crimes together. She definitely wasn't the killer. Evidence recovered at the crime scene pointed to a man. There were hairs that matched at two of the crime scenes, and the MO matched all three. But that didn't change the fact that she was somehow connected. Stone had a problem with putting her in the role of killer, or even accomplice, but he'd been a cop too long to discount anything.

"She didn't do it," Wright said. "She knows the people or the place; that's just coincidence." They turned and looked at each other; cops didn't believe in coincidences.

"We need to keep an eye on Ms. Neil. She's involved; either she's in on it or she's in danger," Stone said.

"I don't think she's in on it. She'd have to be an excellent actress. She was scared, there's no doubt. And why would she involve us if she were in this up to her pretty little neck?" Wright went on. "I think she's in trouble."

As they arrived back at the precinct Stone said, "She's the key. I don't know how she fits, but once we do, we'll have a better chance of catching this monster. It all comes back to Ms. Neil, I'd bet on it." It wasn't a bet Wright would take. Stone's gut was usually right, and it had saved more than a few lives.

OVER THE NEXT FEW DAYS Rissa jumped at the littlest noises, was on edge, couldn't concentrate on anything, and she didn't know how much more she could take. When she wasn't thinking about someone watching her she was thinking about Detective Stone. He'd made an impression on her; only, she didn't quite know what that impression was. She'd found him fascinating and disturbing at the same time. He was dangerously sexy, but he wasn't someone to cross either. The combination intrigued her.

Matt had shown up at closing time for the last three nights, ever since the phone message, to walk her to her car and follow her home. Then she waited in her locked car until he checked her house. He hated leaving, but she wouldn't let him stay. Nothing out of the ordinary happened, and that made her more nervous than anything—the waiting. She knew something else would happen; the detectives had said as much. They told her so she would be cautious, but all it did was put her on edge.

She was so lost in thoughts of how she was becoming a crazy person that when someone knocked on her door she froze. Okay, maybe she didn't mind the waiting, she thought. There was another knock at the door; then the phone rang. She blindly reached for the phone so she wouldn't have to take her eyes off the door. "Hello," she answered.

"Ms. Neil? This is Detective Stone. I'm at your front door. Do you think you could let me in?"

Rissa walked to the door with the phone still in her hand. "Detective Stone?"

"Could you open the door for me?" he asked again.

Leaving the chain in place, she opened the door, almost dropping the phone in relief when she saw the detective. She undid the chain and opened the door. He was a welcome sight and—if it were possible—even sexier than before. He must have been off duty, she thought. He wasn't wearing his slacks and dress shirt, but Rissa wished he had been. Now he had on snug jeans, boots, and a jean jacket. He should have looked out of place in her feminine living room, but he somehow looked natural being there.

"I'm sorry I scared you," Stone apologized once he saw her ashen complexion.

"I'm okay." But her voice betrayed her. "What can I do for you, Detective?"

"Call me Stone."

"Stone? Don't you have a first name?"

"Yeah, but no one calls me by it." He liked the way she had of tilting her head to the side when she was curious.

"Why? Is it horrible?"

"No," he said with a chuckle, "it's Scott. I've just always been called Stone."

"Okay, Stone. Is everything all right?"

"Everything is fine. I just wanted to touch base since it's been a couple of days since we talked. I wanted to see if anything else has come to mind." *What am I doing here?* he asked himself; he could have called, should have called. He knew why he was here; he couldn't get her out of his mind. Coming here tonight wasn't going to help him quit thinking about her, he realized

"I was about to watch the news and have a late dinner. Would you like something?"

"Just coffee, if you don't mind."

"Of course. I'm grateful for the company," she said with slight chagrin. They both knew she didn't like to admit it, but why hide the obvious?

He looked around her living room while she was in the kitchen. He noticed she had several photos hanging on her wall and walked over to look at them. There were some of Rissa with an older woman. Stone thought the resemblance was too uncanny for it not to be her mother. There was one of Rissa and a slightly younger woman standing in front of Rissa's store. But most of them were of Rissa and Matt. While none of them were romantic in any way, they spoke of a closeness the two shared. Stone found himself wondering, not for the first time, what the relationship between Rissa and Matt really was.

"Here you go." She handed him a cup of coffee then sat down in a recliner with a bowl of some kind of noodle dish. He sat down on the couch, and they turned their attention to the news, but it was hard for Stone to concentrate with her sitting so close to him. He could smell her perfume; it was subtle and feminine and reminded him of flowers. She was perfectly proportioned as far as he could tell, but he would rather do some hands-on investigating before he made a final decision.

Her gasp pulled him from his thoughts. At first he had the ridiculous notion that she had read his mind. He could feel himself start to blush for the first time in his adult life, but his embarrassment quickly vanished when he saw her face. Her eyes were fixed on the TV.

"To recap our top story, Ivan Bickerstaff was found dead in his condo by his estranged son Kristof. Kristof states that his father had called him after three years of silence and never said anything, but Caller ID identified his dad's number. The victim, Ivan Bickerstaff, is the owner of Gems by Bickerstaff, a high-end jewelry store that creates one-of-a-kind jewelry designs highly sought after by the rich and famous. Authorities aren't ruling out attempted burglary since Bickerstaff was known to bring his work home occasionally. Kristof was taken to the station for questioning. We don't know yet if he's a suspect or a material witness; authorities aren't releasing any information at this time. We will have more on this story as it develops."

Rissa was shaking. "Rissa, are you okay?" Stone was on his haunches in front of her recliner. "Talk to me. Do you know him?" Stone gave her a little shake when she didn't immediately respond. Rissa blinked a few times, her eyes focusing on Stone. There were tears in her eyes. Stone wanted to comfort her, but he needed answers first. "Rissa, talk to me."

"Ivan." Her voice cracked. "Ivan and my mother dated for years. They almost married, but Kristof threatened to never speak to his dad again if they did. At fifteen he was full of hate and blamed his dad for his mom leaving. Kristof always fantasized that his mom would come back and felt that if Ivan married my mom his dream would never happen. He found out later that his mom didn't want him in her life. But Kristof still blamed Ivan and cut him out of his life anyway. Ivan was a good man; he made Mom happy. It broke her heart when they agreed to end their relationship."

"They agreed?" Stone asked incredulously.

"Ivan only had Kristof; Mom only had me. She knew what it would do to her if I cut her out of my life. She couldn't let that happen to Ivan." Rissa paused, looked up at Stone, and burst out in tears. Stone gathered her in his arms, sat her on his lap, and let her cry. She eventually fell asleep with him holding her. He carried her to bed, covered her up, grabbed the extra pillow, found a blanket on the back of a chair, and headed for the couch. He didn't want her to wake up alone. He knew he wouldn't be able to sleep anytime soon, so he got out his phone and started making calls; he wanted to know exactly how Mr. Bickerstaff had been killed.

Rissa woke the next morning with a splitting headache. She braced her hands on each side of the sink and bowed her head. She couldn't believe Ivan was gone. Even though they hadn't been in contact for years, she remembered him for making her mom happy and knew that she had loved him.

Rissa looked at her puffy eyes. *That's what you get for crying yourself to sleep,* she thought. Rissa froze. With sudden clarity she remembered she hadn't just cried herself to sleep; Stone held her until she feel asleep.

"Oh, how embarrassing!" she moaned. "How can I face him again?" She hoped it would be a long time before she had to. Maybe by then her humiliation would diminish. Disgusted with herself, Rissa started the shower so the water would warm up as she went to start the coffee.

As she turned the corner she froze; there was someone lying on her couch. For a moment she had the thought to turn and run. Then she came to her senses—it had to be Matt. He was concerned when he saw the news and came over. Since he had a key, that made more sense than a killer sleeping on her couch.

"Wake up, sleepyhead!" Rissa said as she came around the recliner. The man looking back at her wasn't Matt, but Stone, and he looked grumpy. Rissa knew from experience that the couch was not comfortable.

"Please tell me you have coffee," Stone grumbled.

"What are you doing here?"

"I didn't want to leave you alone after the shock you had last night." He noticed that her eyes were swollen from crying but knew enough not to mention it. "Well, coffee?"

"Do you always camp on your—" She searched for a word; she wasn't a suspect, victim, or witness. "Do you always camp on women's couches when they are upset?" she finished lamely.

He smiled, and dang it, he looked even sexier. "No, no, I don't. But I'm usually not around when women have another person in a string of many people they know die. I'm usually not the one who holds them when they cry or the one left to put them to bed." Her face burned with embarrassment. "Please, I would kill for a cup of coffee," Stone begged.

Grateful for the change of subject, she smiled. "How do you take your coffee? Oh, dang!" Rissa turned and ran into her room with Stone right behind her.

He caught up to her in her bathroom, turning off her shower. She gave a little yelp when she turned and bumped into him. "I'm sorry! I remembered I turned the shower on to warm up. It doesn't take long for the water to go from cold to hot and back to cold." She was rambling and they both knew it. She turned pink and tried to push past him, but he was like a brick wall. She looked up at him, he grinned at her, causing shivers to race up and down her spine.

"Are you cold?" he asked quietly, his voice still thick with sleep.

"No." Her voice was unusually thick and had nothing to do with having just woken up. She swallowed hard.

He smiled again; they both knew it wasn't cold that made her shiver. He rubbed a thumb across her jaw line, gave a little sigh, and moved aside. She stood there for a second, intrigued by what would happen if she didn't move, but instead she turned and made her escape. What was wrong with her? She wasn't some horny teenager! As she was berating herself, she had no way of knowing that he was having similar thoughts.

Stone sighed out of sheer pleasure as he took his first drink of coffee. Rissa's coffee was almost gourmet compared to the swill they had at the stationhouse. "By the way, I've got some news to share with you, but neither of us has time right now. Are you free tonight?" He smiled at the look of skepticism on her face. "I'd like to go over some notes on the case and see if they jog any memories. I can bring Detective Wright with me if you feel the need for a chaperone."

Rissa laughed. "I'm free tonight. I work until close, and Matt usually escorts me home."

"Why don't I take you to work and pick you up? That way Matt gets a night off and we can talk some on the way there."

Rissa couldn't see any reason to protest, so she agreed. She took extra time with her hair and makeup and picking out her clothes. *Why do I pick now, of all times, to start noticing men again? And Stone, of all men?* she asked herself as she headed down the hall.

After promising to pick her up at closing time, Stone watched her get safely in the store before pulling away. A couple minutes after being dropped off, Rissa couldn't help but smile as she realized Stone never mentioned anything about the case.

Rissa suddenly got a chill down her spine; it was as if she could feel someone watching her. She slowly looked around the store but didn't see anyone. She tried to shake off the feeling, chalking it up to her imagination, and got to work.

"STONE, YOU LOOK A LITTLE worse for wear," Wright said affably. "Late night?"

"What?" Stone asked defensively. He shook his head and said, "We have a new lead."

"What might that be, partner?" Wright didn't know what had just happened but wasn't the type to dwell on it.

"Ivan Bickerstaff was murdered last night. His murder might be connected to our cases."

"Yeah? I heard about that; what makes you think there's a connection?" Wright asked around a bite of donut.

"Turns out, Rissa Neil knew the vic. I called the Mason County Police, where the murder took place. The MO is the same. They were a little perturbed by that news since they were sure the son was good for it and figured it was a slam dunk. But the son had been out of the state recently and wasn't here during one of our murders, so if the murders are all related, that leaves him in the clear."

"You've been busy," Wright said, stuffing the rest of his second—or was it his third—donut into his mouth. Washing it down with a cup of horrible stationhouse coffee he asked, "How'd you get on this so fast?"

"I went by to check on Ms. Neil, and while I was there the news came on." Stone watched his partner, but if he seemed to think anything was odd about him going to see her, he didn't show it. "She saw the story and filled me in on how she knew the vic, and once I got a chance, I did some checking."

They spent the next couple of hours checking backgrounds and checking for known acquaintances for anyone else they might have had in common other than Rissa.

"What was the name of the couple Rissa said had lived in the house the Youngs were killed in?" Stone asked, breaking the long silence.

"Let's see." Wright flipped through his notes. "Bennington, Steve and Ariel."

"Put their name on our chart beside the Youngs's name. I don't think the Youngs were the intended targets. They're the only ones that we can't link back to Rissa, but the previous occupants can be. Let's see if Rissa has the current number and address of the Benningtons." Wright smiled; he didn't miss that Stone had called Rissa by her first name. Stone didn't notice the smile as he reached for the phone to call Rissa. Nor did he notice that the smile turned into an intrigued look when he didn't need to look up the number and he knew exactly where she was.

"It's Stone," Stone said neutrally when Rissa answered, aware that Wright was paying close attention. "Do you have current contact information for the Benningtons?"

"Hold on a second; let me grab my purse." Coming back to the phone, Rissa said, "I don't see my address book. Dang it, I know it's here." She continued to rummage while Stone waited. "I don't know, Stone; it isn't here. It's always in my purse, but it's possible I left it at home."

"Don't worry. I'll look them up through the DMV. I'll see you later." He hung up and caught Wright smiling at him. "What?"

"Nothing." Wright said then started humming the K-I-S-S song that school kids sing.

"Kiss off, Wright!" Stone snarled. Wright laughed.

RISSA WAS TIRED BY THE time Stone came to get her. It had been a long and busy day. She sniffed the air as she got in his truck.

"Chinese," Stone said. "I figured we could work while we eat. I'm starving."

"Sounds good to me. I haven't had a chance to eat a decent meal today. Things were hectic today."

"How's that?" Stone was interested in anything that seemed out of the ordinary to Rissa.

"Oh, the normal kind of hectic: 'I forgot the wife's/girlfriend's/mom's/sister's birthday' type of hectic. We have those every now and then. The frantic male comes rushing in, needing a present to make up for a forgotten birthday of his loved one, and he needs it yesterday. I don't know why men seem to have so much trouble remembering dates."

"So nothing unusual happened today?" Stone asked, ignoring the apt description of most of the men on the face of the planet.

"There was this one guy who wanted a present for his girlfriend. When I asked him what she liked, he said, 'Pick something you would like.' I tried to get some personal information like favorite flower, favorite color—you know, trying to get a feel for the girlfriend. But he'd just repeat, 'Whatever you like.' To top it off, he mumbled and was hard to understand."

"What did he end up getting her?" Stone asked.

"Lilac perfume and a beaded purse that I've been eyeing for myself. I hope she likes my taste as much as he seems to think she will!" Rissa laughed, Stone didn't.

Stone mulled over what Rissa had told him for the remainder of the drive. Rissa didn't seem to mind the silence; she closed her eyes and leaned her head back. She hadn't breathed easy all day. The creepy feeling she'd gotten that morning had stayed with her. She'd felt like a bow drawn tight and ready to break any minute. She knew she had to get a grip, but when you didn't know what was going on, how could you get a grip on it?

"We're here," Stone said, watching her as she slowly opened her eyes.

"Wow! That didn't take long, did it?"

"Come on; let's get inside. I'm starving." Stone grabbed the bags of Chinese food and his briefcase. His eyes didn't settle as they walked to the front door. He was constantly scanning the area, looking for anything odd, so he was the first to notice something on her doorstep. "Are you expecting any deliveries?" Stone asked, pulling up short.

"No. I don't have anything delivered to the house; everything I order, even personal, goes to the store." Rissa was standing close enough to feel his muscles flex. He handed the food to her and nudged her behind him. From where she was she couldn't see anything, nor could she see Stone's hand resting on the butt of his gun.

She peeked around his shoulder to see a bouquet of roses resting against her door. "Oh, who would send me flowers?"

She didn't notice that the question sparked Stone's interest until he turned to her and asked, "Yes, who would send you flowers?"

Understanding dawned, and a terrified look came across her face. In a small voice she asked, "You don't think 'he' sent me flowers, do you?"

"Well, you brought up a great point when you asked who. Would Matt send you flowers?" She had no idea how interested he was in the answer to that question. He felt as though she and Matt were more than friends, and it irritated him.

"He could have, but never roses. He usually sends me some sunny type of arrangement and then only on special occasions. I could see him sending something to cheer me up, but again, not roses." She thought for a second then added, "No, it isn't from Matt. He knows I never get home early, and he knows you were picking me up tonight. He would have sent them to me at work, I'm positive!"

"Anyone come to mind—an ex or someone who's asked you out lately?" Stone took hold of her arm and put her between him and the house, blocking her from any prying eyes or lucky shots. Rissa gave a negative shake of her head in answer to his question. "Let's get inside and try to figure this out. I don't like standing here in the open; whoever left them might be watching to see your reaction." He bent down and grabbed the flowers as they walked in the front door. Stone set the flowers on the table in the entryway.

"I don't see a card."

"I don't either, and there's no florist's sticker on it, either. That means they weren't delivered by the florist. He delivered them himself." Stone carried the flowers into the kitchen. Laying them on the counter, he unrolled the green paper they were in and spread the stems out. "No, there's no card. What do you want to do with them?" He turned to see her holding out a small kitchen trashcan. He smiled at her as he swiped them off the counter into the trashcan.

"Let's eat," Rissa said as she set the trashcan down.

Stone admired her ability to handle stress, and possibly getting flowers from someone wishing you harm was a huge stressor. "Eating is good, but I need to call Wright first. I want him to be aware of the flowers and see if he has anything new." Stone, pulling his cell phone out to call Wright, gave Rissa a reassuring smile. "We will find out who—" His comment was interrupted when Wright apparently answered the phone. Stone turned and walked into the other room.

"Wright, I'm at Rissa Neil's." Stone tightened his jaw at the chuckle he heard on the other end of the line. "Knock it off, Wright. There were some roses left for Rissa on her doorstep. No card, no florist mark, nothing identifiable. They were your standard red roses and more than likely, untraceable. They are in a plastic trash bag right now, but I'll bring them in tomorrow for forensics to look over just in case I've missed something. They had to have been delivered by the perp himself. Let's get some patrolmen out here in the morning and question the neighbors. Maybe someone saw something."

"There is nothing threatening about roses; well, unless you're being stalked. Is there a possibility they are from her friend Matt?" Wright asked in a mumbled voice. Stone knew he had caught his partner while he was eating, which was most of the time. Wright was a good man, but he wasn't in good shape. He would never make it through a physical, and he'd probably have a heart attack if he had to chase a suspect.

"She is sure Matt wouldn't send roses, and she never has anything delivered to the house. Those two are pretty tight, so I would say on points like this, Rissa would know best." Stone paused. Wright waited knowing Stone wasn't done. "You know, I'm going to have Rissa call Matt and ask. There is something about him that bothers me."

"Can't hurt."

"All right, call if you hear anything, and I'll do the same." Stone hung up before getting a response. Wright was used to Stone having a one-track mind on a case and wasn't the least bit offended.

Stone went back into the kitchen to see that Rissa had gotten them iced tea and plates for the Chinese food, but she hadn't touched the food yet. She was sitting at the table staring at the small trashcan. She turned, smiling at him as he came in.

"Everything okay?"

"Fine. He'll call if he gets anything new. After dinner I would like you to give Matt a call and just make sure he didn't leave you the roses." Before she could interrupt he continued. "I know you said you are positive it wasn't him, but it would make me feel better if we at least asked. Who knows, maybe he did and has a logical explanation for why he left them on your steps instead of bringing them to the store. Maybe they were running a sale on roses…I don't know, but humor me."

"Okay, it's easy enough to check and cross that off the list at least."

"Let's eat," Stone said, sitting down at the table.

The dinner was delicious, but Rissa's eyes kept going back to the roses sticking out of the top of the small trashcan. Stone got up, tied the trash bag closed, took the bag out of the can, and set it out of sight. "After dinner, I'll put them in my truck. I want to take them with me tomorrow in case there is something we missed when we looked at them." Rissa gave him a small smile and visibly relaxed as he sat back down.

When dinner was over, Stone and Rissa got settled in the living room. "We need to run through things again. I need you to start from the beginning and bring it up to date. Don't leave anything out, no matter how insignificant it seems. I won't interrupt, but once you're done I'll have questions. We'll run through it several times. The more you go over something, the more you might remember something new."

Rissa sighed. "Sounds like it's going to be a long night." She told Stone about losing her mom two years earlier and how she had thrown herself into work, how Matt and Tina were the only ones who had stayed by her side. She went over the night at work when she had felt someone watching her—how she had been scared enough she dropped her purse and scattered everything in it all over the pavement. How she could have sworn she saw a figure step out of the bushes, but once she got into her car and aimed her headlights toward the area, there was nothing there. She told him about coming home and calling Matt and about going for a car ride to his house in the country the next day. She told him how the following day she had heard on the radio about her old friend Teresa Abner being killed.

"Then nothing for about a week. Then I heard on the news about Mindi Andrews. A few days after that there was the news about the killing at a house of some people I know. While the Benningtons don't still live there, it's a huge coincidence that I would know them with all that has been going on."

She then told him about needing some time off and Tina covering for her and about the calls Tina had received while she was gone. She told Stone about Matt's announcement of his upcoming nuptials and the celebration.

"The next day was horrible because of all of the alcohol I had consumed while celebrating. The phone rang a couple of times that morning, but I needed coffee, aspirin, and a shower and let the machine pick it up. That's when I got the message that got you involved. I called Matt, and once he heard it, he called you.

"Nothing happened after that until you were here and I heard the news of Ivan. That brings us up to today. You took me to work, and I got this creepy feeling like I was being watched. It has stayed with me all day."

"Okay, now for some questions." They spent the next two hours picking her story apart to see if they could get anything new out of it.

"So now we know some things we didn't before. When you dropped your purse and things scattered everywhere, you aren't one hundred percent sure you gathered everything up. In fact, you stated that you knew you were leaving stuff on the ground because you were too scared of whoever was in the bushes coming after you." Stone couldn't help but think to himself that she took a huge risk stopping to pick anything up. She should have left everything and gotten herself safely locked in her car. Instead of saying any of that he went on. "You've most likely been watched for some time before you even realized it. While you don't have many friends you see often, the ones you do have are irreplaceable. And I think you are the link between these murders."

Rissa's mouth dropped open, but nothing came out. His words were painful to hear even though she had come to the same conclusion herself. But to hear it out loud was completely different. The phone rang before she could figure out how to respond.

"Hello," Rissa answered distractedly.

"Hey, honey, how's it going? I figured you would call me when you got home, but I was getting worried."

Since she was distracted it took a moment to realize it was Matt on the phone. "Oh, Matt, I'm sorry I didn't call. I was going to right after dinner, then Detective Stone and I started going over the case, and I forgot…I'm sorry. I should've called."

"Are you okay?" His concern was evident.

"Of course. As I said, Detective Stone's here."

"I heard that, but you sound upset. Has something else happened?"

"No, not really, well, that's not true." Rissa swallowed hard. "Matt, did you leave flowers for me on my doorstep tonight?"

"No, I didn't. What's going on?" Matt asked.

"When we got home tonight there were some roses on my doorstep. There was no card and Detective Stone wanted to verify they weren't from you."

"You know that's not something I would do."

"I know, but it never hurts to ask, right?" Rissa thought Matt's voice sounded strange.

"No, no, you're right. The detective doesn't know me, and he should question everyone and everything. I guess it just bothered me to think you would question me, but I can see that it isn't you asking; it's the detective. I get it." Matt changed the subject. "Is that the only thing bothering you? You sounded upset when you answered the phone."

"We've been rehashing events, and it's been a little upsetting. I'm okay, I promise."

"That reminds me, did you find out who left the rose on your car?" Matt asked.

"No, I forgot about that."

"Be sure to tell the detective."

"I will," Rissa assured him.

"Well, call me if you need me." Matt sounded reluctant to hang up.

"Of course."

"I love you."

Rissa smiled and got tears in her eyes. "I love you too, Matt. I'll call if I need you."

"Even if you don't need me, call me whenever you want. I can be there in a jiffy."

She didn't notice that Stone had been tuned in to every word she said. It wasn't that he thought of Matt as a suspect, but he didn't like the closeness they shared. He knew she was in love with him and figured that Matt was in love with her too. Why did they insist that they weren't a couple? If they were a couple, why wasn't Matt here? Stone thought that if it was his woman in trouble he wouldn't let her out of his sight. Stone didn't think much of Matt.

"Matt assures me that he didn't leave the roses," Rissa said, breaking into Stone's thoughts.

"I didn't really think so, but thanks for checking."

"He did remind me that I received a rose on my windshield at work right after the incident in the parking lot."

"That strengthens the scenario of the perp following and watching you."

Rissa took a deep breath and got back to the subject they were on before the phone call. "So how're the cases linked to me?" Rissa asked.

As interested as he was in her and Matt's relationship, he had to concentrate on the case. Getting back to the original subject, he said, "Other than the MOs being the same, you're the only link we have between these crimes. The victims are from different walks of life. None of them run in the same circles, are in the same income bracket, or live the same lifestyle. You're the only common denominator." Stone paused, going over his notes. "Since dropping your purse, have you noticed anything missing?"

"Not that I can think of," Rissa answered.

"Are you sure? Didn't you mention earlier that you couldn't find your address book?"

"Yeah, I usually keep it in my purse, and I don't remember taking it out. But I haven't had a chance to look for it yet."

"Why don't we look now? I have a theory, and if I'm right, we might be able to save some lives." With a comment like that, Rissa started tearing her house apart looking for the book. Stone didn't know what it looked like, but he was searching everywhere he could think of. If it was a book, he looked in it to see if it could be the missing address book. After a thorough look around the house and Rissa's car, there was no address book.

"Okay, it isn't anywhere to be found. Now what?"

"I think whoever was watching you leave work that night found your address book in the parking lot."

"Okay, so…what does that mean?" Rissa wasn't following.

"Take a look at the names of the victims: Abner, Andrews, Bennington, Bickerstaff. They go in alphabetical order. In an order that you would have them listed in your address book."

"Isn't that a stretch? That's quite an assumption with only four names to go on, and the Benningtons don't even live there anymore. That ruins your theory, doesn't it?" Oh, how she hoped it ruined his theory.

"Yes, it's an assumption, but I'd rather not wait for more names to be added before we act on it. And it only blows my theory if—and it's an important if—you changed your friends' address in the book. If you hadn't changed the address, it would show that they still lived there."

Stone could see Rissa's mind working, trying to recall what was in her address book. He knew the answer by the look of distress on her face—she hadn't changed it. So if he was correct, the only reason the Youngs were killed was because they bought a house.

Rissa sat there shaking her head, tears running down her face. He got up and knelt in front of her. "Believe it or not, this is good news. It's a tangible lead. You're going to have to try to recreate your address book so we can warn people, but it's a step in the right direction. It's a lot more than we had."

"All because of me?" she said to herself. "This is all because of me."

"No, it isn't. Listen to me, Rissa. This isn't your fault! Do you understand that? If he hadn't gotten hold of your address book, he would have found another way. This isn't your fault; it's his! He's the one doing this, not you. He's fixated on you. We don't know why, but that's another piece to the puzzle. We'll find him and stop him."

He pulled her into his arms and let her cry. He sat there, knowing he was getting in too deep and there was nothing he could do about it. She might be in love with someone else, but Matt wasn't here, he was. He couldn't sit there and watch her in pain and not do anything about it. He'd just have to deal with his feelings when the time came. Rissa was already under his skin.

CHAPTER 3

ONCE AGAIN RISSA WOKE WITH a splitting headache from crying herself to sleep. She got in the shower, knowing Stone was still there without checking. How had he become so important so fast? How had he managed to get in her head when she hadn't noticed a man in two years? It was as if she'd been sleepwalking and woke up to the sexiest, most fascinating man she had ever met. Her mind kept going back to Stone, and that led her back to their conversation the previous night. She was the link to these murders? None of it made sense. She hadn't done anything for someone to want to do this to her and those she loved. She got out of the shower as it started getting cold. Sitting on the edge of the tub wrapped in a towel, she tried to get things figured out.

She was still sitting there when Stone walked in. He'd listened to her moving around and had heard the water running through the pipes as she took a shower. He'd given her plenty of time to get dressed, and she still hadn't made an appearance. He poured her some coffee and went in to check on her. He found her sitting on the edge of the tub holding her head, wearing nothing but a fluffy, blue towel. She felt him watching her and lifted her head. Her eyes were bruised from crying, and she was pale. She took a deep breath, causing him to notice the swell of her breasts that was visible above the towel.

"I brought you coffee," he said huskily, trying to keep his eyes on hers.

Rissa took a tentative sip since she liked her coffee a particular way. She was surprised it was perfect. She looked up at him. Reading her surprised look, he grinned. "I'm a detective. I'm paid to notice details."

"Thank you. And thank you for being my protector again last night while I slept."

"No problem, but if this becomes a habit, I want better sleeping conditions." He could tell she jumped to conclusions, but interestingly enough, he also noticed the pulse in her neck beat faster. Her breathing sped up, causing his eyes to go back to the swell of her breasts. He hadn't meant it in any way but wanting a more comfortable place to sleep, but the thought was intriguing.

"You have a spare room; is the bed any more comfortable than the couch?" he asked as if he hadn't noticed her reaction, but the thickness of his voice betrayed him. Taking a drink of his coffee, he watched her over the rim of the mug. She was blushing, and he wondered if the rest of her was too.

"Umm...I don't know. I've never slept on it, but it has to be better than the couch. The floor is better than the couch. I've been meaning to buy a new one but haven't gotten around to it." She was rambling but couldn't help it. The state of her undress must have come to her attention, because she kept trying to pull it up to cover herself, causing her to show more of her legs than Stone could stand. He knew if she pulled the towel up any higher she would be uncovering other interesting places; only, she didn't realize she was doing it. Stone was trying not to wonder how she would look without the towel.

He decided to give her a break and knew if he stayed there any longer his curiosity would get the better of him. "I'll wait in the other room."

She stared at the empty doorway for a moment, smiling. If he could've read her mind he might not have left the room so willingly. When he mentioned the "better sleeping conditions" her mind had gone places it had never gone before. The look on his face said he had some interesting ideas of his own. She wasn't the type that acted out on physical attractions foolishly. She'd never felt any physical attraction strong enough to move forward blindly, but she'd come close for the first time in her life. If he'd stayed any longer she was afraid she would have reached out to him.

MAYBE IT WAS THE WAY his thoughts had taken him earlier, but he couldn't remember wanting a woman as much as he wanted her. *This is work* was his mantra as he refilled his coffee.

"So,"—she looked at him defiantly—"what do we do now?"

Stone admired her spunk. "Well, I've been thinking about that. First, you need to try to recreate your address book—" The phone interrupted him.

"I better get that. It might be Matt, and if I don't answer he might show up with guns blazing." Stone absently wondered if Matt owned any guns and if they were licensed.

"Hello?" Rissa listened for a moment before she started yelling. "Who are you? What do you want?"

Stone was instantly at her side, taking the phone. "Who is this?"

"Leave her alone; she's mine!" a voice hissed, and then the phone went dead.

Stone hung up and turned to take her into his arms, holding her until the shaking stopped. He eased her back, and instead of the tears he expected, he saw pure, raw anger. She was all but vibrating with it.

"Are you okay? What'd he say?"

She reluctantly moved away from him. She knew she had to be strong to face this, and if she let Stone be her crutch she would never be able to see this through. She took a deep breath. "He said he knew I had a man in my bed last night. He said I belonged to him." Her voice hitched a little.

"Did you recognize the voice?"

"It was the same person who left the message before; I'm sure of it."

"I think so too. He warned me away from you, said you were his." Stone put a hand on each of her shoulders, his thumbs rubbing the pulse on her neck. "I need you to call Matt; tell him you're coming to the country house to spend the day." Before she could interrupt, he went on. "I need to go fill in the captain and Wright. I can't leave you here alone, and I don't want you to go to work. I want you to be with someone you trust, never alone." He hated sending her to Matt—he didn't want her anywhere near him—but her safety was more important. If keeping her alive meant he risked losing his chance with her, then that's the way it would be.

She started to say something then stopped. "All right, we'll do it your way. After all, you're the professional. But I have one question: how will I get out of here without him following me? He's watching me, and I don't want to be vulnerable on the long drive out to the country house. I don't want to involve Matt in this. What if he gets hurt?"

Stone sat her down and kneeled in front of her. "Matt wouldn't appreciate you trying to keep him out of this, for one thing. If he knows what's going on, he's less likely to do something stupid; he'll be better prepared. As for you getting out of town, I've got an idea. I'll have a female officer take an unmarked car to a parking garage, and the two of you will switch places. He won't see the switch; the garage we use is a high-security garage, and you have to have special credentials to use it. Once the switch is made you can take that car to the country. We've had to do it before in cases where we needed to hide a witness; it's always been successful."

Rissa smiled, reached up, and gave him a quick kiss. It was a small kiss, one you would give a friend, but it surprised them both. "Sorry," she said, blushing. "I'm just thankful not to be in this alone."

Stone smiled at her and brushed his thumb lightly across her lips. "You aren't alone, and there's no need to apologize. It wasn't too terrible."

"Not too terrible, huh?" She laughed as he had intended, but it took all his self-control not to grab her and give her a real kiss. His mind played with the idea for a second; if he gave her something to think about while she was out there with Matt, he might be able to give the rich boy a run for his money. He turned to gather his stuff before he acted on his thoughts.

While Rissa made her phone call to Matt, Stone called the department and made plans for the switch. Done at the same time Stone asked, "Ready?"

"As I'll ever be."

THE SWITCH WENT OFF WITHOUT a hitch. Since leaving the garage, Rissa had been watching the rearview mirror to see if she was being followed. There were long stretches of road where she could see for miles, but that didn't keep her from worrying.

She jumped when her cell phone rang. "Hello."

"Hey, I wanted to make sure you were doing okay." Rissa smiled at hearing Stone's voice.

"Yeah, I'm good. I can't seem to quit watching the rearview mirror, though." Other than worrying that someone might be following her, Stone was the only thing she could think about. When they said goodbye at the garage, Stone had leaned over and given her a quick kiss. Rissa was sure the surprise on her face matched the surprise on his. He hadn't meant to kiss her. He'd been thinking about it though, and without realizing what he was doing, he reached over and kissed her. As she got out of Stone's truck she got an approving wink from the female officer. Rissa, her face burning, smiled shyly and got in the SUV waiting for her and drove off.

"Watching the rearview mirror isn't a bad thing," Stone said, bringing Rissa out of her reminiscing. "It's better to be cautious."

"Then consider me very cautious."

Stone chuckled. "How long until you're there?"

"About ten minutes."

"I take it Matt's anxiously waiting?" he said in an odd tone.

"Laura's gone with the symphony, and Matt said he could use the company. She left this morning, and he doesn't know what to do with himself. He's a goner." Rissa laughed.

"Sounds like it," he said flatly.

Rissa wasn't sure what was wrong. "Have you talked to the captain yet?"

"Not yet. He's in a meeting with the DA."

"How long will I have to stay at Matt's?"

No longer than necessary, Stone thought, but he said, "I don't know yet. I'll know more after I talk to Wright and the captain. Look, he's motioning to me now. I have to go."

"Okay."

"Rissa?"

"Yes?"

There was a long silence. Then he simply said, "Be safe," and hung up.

Rissa wondered what he'd really wanted to say. But the thought disappeared as she reached Matt's house and saw him waiting for her.

IT WAS A DAUNTING JOB trying to re-create an address book she'd had for years. She had lost touch with so many people over time she was afraid she wouldn't be able to remember half of them. Matt could only help so much; the rest was up to her.

Stone hadn't called by nine that night, and Rissa knew she would be staying the night. She'd stayed there before, but she didn't like that she wouldn't be seeing Stone. Would she see him when this was all over? After all, this was a job to him. That thought bothered her more than she wanted to admit.

That evening, Matt and Rissa sat in front of the fireplace with his arm around her and her head resting on his shoulder. Stone saw the cozy scene when he looked in the window as he stepped on the porch. Jealousy hit him hard. He couldn't accept that a man and woman could be that close without having a sexual relationship. At least, he'd never had that kind of relationship.

Matt got up to answer the knock at the door as Rissa held her breath. It was late to be getting a visitor, especially this far out. She was pleasantly surprised to see Stone standing there.

"Stone!" Rissa exclaimed happily before she noticed his expression.

Stone and Matt shook hands, but the look on Stone's face was anything but pleasant. Rissa feared the worst. "What's happened? Why are you here?"

Not hearing the fear, Stone took her questions to mean she didn't want him there. The look on his face became harder; she didn't think it was possible. Rissa, thinking someone else had died, started shaking.

"I'm sorry for interrupting," Stone said, not looking at Rissa.

"Don't be stupid, come in." Matt wasn't sure what was going on, but he felt the anger radiating off Stone.

"Has someone else been hurt?"

"No. I just thought I'd—" The sentence died when he finally looked at Rissa. Softening his voice, he said, "I wanted to see if you were all right. I'm sorry; I didn't mean to scare you." Stone didn't know what was going on, but he knew she was scared, not angry. He was confused by his reaction and by hers. It went against everything they had told him about their relationship, but still…

Matt, sensing they needed privacy, quietly left the room. Neither of them seemed to notice. He looked back as he went into his room for the night and smiled. "Good night," he called, but they didn't give any indication of hearing him. They were just staring at each other.

When Stone heard the door close he cleared his throat. "I'm sorry if I interrupted the two of you."

Rissa didn't know what he meant by that and tilted her head questioningly, the way Stone found so endearing. When Stone didn't respond to her unspoken question, understanding slowly dawned on her. "There's nothing to interrupt, I swear. Matt and I have never been anything but friends."

"You don't have to explain—" Stone started, but Rissa spoke over him.

"Yes, I do. I have to make you understand that he's my best friend and I love him dearly. We're close, and he's lost several girlfriends because of our relationship. They never believed we could be so close and there not be more between us, but they were wrong. Matt finally found someone who understands." Rissa looked at Stone, pleading with her eyes for understanding.

"It'd be easier if you weren't so affectionate with each other. Your voice softens when you talk about him and he calls you 'honey' and 'baby' and 'sweetheart.' It seems so…oh never mind. I don't have any right to judge your relationship; we just met." Stone's aggravation was palpable.

Rissa walked to him, put her hands on his shoulder, and pulled him down to her for a kiss, a real kiss. There was a low growl from Stone as he wrapped his arms around her waist and lifted her off her feet, deepening the kiss.

Coming up for air, she said, "You have every right if that kiss is any indication of how you feel about me. Just so you know, I'd like to get to know you better. There's nothing between me and anybody else that should worry you." Stone sat her on her feet and framed her face with his hands.

"I don't know what it is about you, but you've gotten past my defenses faster than anyone I've ever known. I'm not the jealous type, but when I saw you two together I saw red."

Rissa smiled, laying her head on his chest. As he held her, he could hear the laughter in her voice when she said, "When we first met he started calling me 'sweet cakes' all the time. He knew I hated it, and it made it all the more fun for him. It went on for so long that it stuck, and eventually I quit minding the nicknames.

"I bet that didn't help his girlfriends understand your relationship."

Rissa laughed. "No, not at all." The laughter gone, she added, "They all pulled some version of the 'it's her or me' thing. I never wanted to cause problems with him and his love life. I suggested he not call me those types of names; you see how that worked."

"As I can attest, it's hard to understand your relationship, and the nicknames don't help." Her chuckle was her only reply. Then she looked up at him, and he knew he was a goner. His head dipped, and he kissed her, hoping he'd be as understanding about Rissa's and Matt's relationship as Matt's fiancée was.

"YOU HAVE AN UNFAIR ADVANTAGE."

"How's that?"

"You know a lot about me, and I don't know anything about you."

"What would you like to know?" Stone asked.

"I don't know. Um, where'd you grow up? Do you have siblings? Are your parents still around? Why a police officer? How old are you? Have you ever been married? Engaged?"

"Wow, for someone who doesn't know what to ask, you sure have a lot of questions." Stone laughed. He had a nice laugh. It was deep and warm; she liked the sound of it. They were sitting on the couch, almost exactly like she had sat with Matt, only it didn't feel innocent. Not with some of the mind-blowing kisses they'd shared.

"Well, let's see...Where'd I grow up? Georgia, until I was eleven; then we moved to Texas to be near my grandfather. He had a small ranch and needed help to take care of it." He absently rubbed Rissa's back as he spoke. "Second question, siblings: I have a younger brother named Jacob, and I have two sisters, Lily, who is the oldest, and Stacey. Stacey's the baby." There was so much affection when he spoke of his family that Rissa felt a pang of envy for something she didn't, and would never, have. "What was the next question?"

"Are your parents still around?"

"Dad was killed in a drive-by shooting when I was fifteen," Stone said matter-of-factly. "That answers another question: why a police officer? The officer that solved Dad's case was a good man. He helped my family come to terms with our loss." Stone paused. "The man who shot Dad was aiming for a couple behind Dad. It was the man's wife and her lover; the affair pushed him over the edge. He didn't hit anyone but my dad." Rissa was silently crying. Stone, feeling her tears soak through his shirt, tipped her chin up and kissed her. "Its okay, baby; we made it through. Johnson, the officer that worked dad's case, helped. He's a good man, and we stay in touch."

Rissa was surprised at how comfortable she was with Stone, at least while they were just sitting there. If he kept kissing her, the comfort level would bottom out. She'd be wise to remember Stone wasn't Matt. "What happened to your grandfather and Officer Johnson?"

"So the inquisition isn't quite over, huh?" Stone asked sleepily, smiling. "Granddad died about ten years after we moved to Texas and Lt. Johnson retired five years ago and lives in Montana."

"What about your mom?"

"She still has the ranch but leases the land to ranchers, and that pays all of her bills. She belongs to several groups and is having the time of her life." Stone yawned. "Are we done yet?"

"Not yet. How old you are? Ever been married?"

"I'm thirty-five and never been married. I came close, but she got wise and took off three weeks before the wedding, said she didn't like my interfering family."

"Are they?"

"Interfering? No. They call on occasion to catch up and want to spend holidays together when possible. Her parents forget they have a daughter half the time, and she wasn't used to a family that actually cared."

"Well, that's stupid! You'd think not having a family would make her appreciate yours." Stone knew she was thinking of her own lack of family and hugged her tightly.

"So, what about—"

"Enough! It's time for bed." He knew by the way she tensed up that she was thinking he meant together.

As they headed toward the room she always claimed as her own when she stayed out at the country house, which wasn't often, she was trying to figure out a way to tell him she wasn't prepared for this. When they reached the bedroom door, he gently turned her toward him, leaned down, and gave her a sweet, gentle kiss.

"Good night, Rissa," Stone said quietly, his deep voice causing butterflies to dance in Rissa's stomach.

She stood there, the feeling of his lips still on hers, and watched him go back to the living room and lay down on the couch. She couldn't help but smile since this was the third time he would sleep on a couch for her.

STONE WANTED RISSA TO STAY at Matt's a few more days to keep her safe while the police went over the list of names she'd made. Rissa didn't like leaving her shop, and he didn't want anyone to know where Rissa was, Tina included.

"But what if they need me at the store? We start our holiday season early in the retail business. The beginning of October isn't all that early for Christmas shoppers. Actually, the busy holiday season has already started, so I need to be at the store."

"Tina can call *me* if she needs *you*," Stone said a little too calmly. "Look, Rissa. I'll be able to concentrate better if I know you're safe and no one knows where you are. You've said that no one but the three of us and Laura knows about this place. You can't get much safer than that. If you call someone and let it slip where you are…" Stone didn't finish since it was the umpteenth time he'd gone over it since bringing the subject up over breakfast. They were still in the kitchen, but Matt was the only one still sitting. He was drinking his coffee, watching the two of them battle it out like it was the Super Bowl and he had a vested interest in who won. Stone was leaning against the counter trying to hold his temper while Rissa paced back and forth, aggravated that she didn't seem to be gaining any ground in the argument.

Rissa stopped directly in front of Stone. "You're a cop, what do you mean 'you can concentrate better'?

Do you hide all your...whatever I am, away?" Rissa thought that was a good argument. He couldn't possibly hide everyone who was involved in his cases.

Stone leaned close to her and said between clenched teeth, "No one else distracts me the way you do. As it is, I will have trouble *not* thinking about you. If I don't know where you are or who's with you, it'll be even worse."

Rissa smiled and threw her arms around him. "Why didn't you say so? Of course I'll stay here."

Stone shook his head and laughed, tightening his hold on Rissa. Looking over the top of Rissa's head, Stone said to Matt, "If only I'd known that's all I had to say."

Matt had stayed out of the conversation when, after agreeing with Stone, Rissa had turned her fiery glare at him. Matt wanted her safe too but felt he would be on safer ground letting Stone do the convincing. At Stone's comment, Rissa turned to look at Matt. He gave her a smile and innocently shrugged. He still refused to comment on the subject, and Rissa couldn't help but smile.

Rissa was as relieved as Stone was that they had finally agreed, or more precisely that she finally agreed with his idea. She still didn't like that she couldn't be at the store and that Tina couldn't reach her. Tina wasn't a threat to her and said as much. Stone replied, "It isn't Tina hurting you that I'm afraid of. If someone trips her up and she lets something slip...I know you two are close, but that's how mistakes happen."

Stone had been gone a couple of hours, and Rissa kept replaying the morning's arguments over in her head. She finally admitted that he had a point, but that didn't mean she had to like it.

THE DAYS CREPT BY SLOWLY without any progress, but on the third day Rissa wished it had stayed that way. That night as Rissa and Matt finished dinner they heard a car drive up. "It looks like you get a personal visit rather than a phone call tonight," Matt said. Rissa brought the dishes she was carrying to the sink and left them in the water as she went to greet Stone. "Don't worry; I'll get the dishes," Matt grumbled.

Rissa threw the door open, her smile fading once she saw Stone and Wright, knowing immediately that something was wrong.

"Hello, Ms. Neil," Wright said.

"Hello, Detective Wright," Rissa said, not taking her eyes off Stone. Shutting the door, Stone led Rissa to the couch. She didn't want to hear what he had to say. She wanted them to leave and come back smiling.

"Rissa,"—Stone stopped at the tears in her eyes. He took a deep breath and started over. "Rissa, we have been trying to contact everyone on your list, but some of the people haven't been home."

Matt took in the looks on everyone's faces as he entered the room and knew it wasn't good. "What's going on?"

"We're just getting to that," Stone said, never looking away from Rissa. "We've contacted almost everyone on your list. They've all temporarily relocated, but it seems the stalker has escalated. We believe that the combination of not finding you and not being able to find the people in your book have angered him. He's gotten inside some of the houses on your list and ransacked the homes when he couldn't find anyone."

"And you're sure it's the same person?" Rissa knew it was, but she couldn't fathom someone hating her that much.

Stone understood. "I checked your answering machine, and there are some very unpleasant messages on it. If we can get a voice match, the SOB will go to jail for some of the things he has threatened alone."

"There's more, isn't there?" Rissa knew Stone wasn't done. She was strong, but Stone didn't know how much more she could take. The worst of the news was yet to come, and he hated having to be the one to tell her.

"As I said, people we talked to went to stay with friends or family. We still kept an eye on their homes and have found several of them ransacked," Stone continued. "Not everyone was home when we tried to contact them, so we posted a man outside those homes." Stone took a ragged breath and exhaled it almost violently. "He killed one of the officers standing watch. He dragged his body into the bushes and waited. A couple of guys—Nathan Rose and Zachary Dane—were killed."

"I don't know Zachary Dane, but Nathan Rose is the contractor I hired to refurbish my store. Are you sure it was connected to me?" Rissa answered her own question. "Of course you're sure, otherwise you wouldn't have mentioned it. I almost didn't add him until Matt asked me about business people I've worked with. I got to running through everyone I used for the store." Looking up at Stone, she continued. "I take it the way they were killed was the same as the others." It was a statement, so no one commented.

"We figure he started jumping around in your address book to have gone after someone with the last name of Rose. R is a long way off from B." After several minutes of silence, Wright cleared his throat, and Rissa knew there was more.

"What else?" *Please, how could it get worse,* Rissa thought.

"As I said, the killer is escalating. He attacked someone else. We were watching her, but the officer lost her at a stoplight. By the time the officer got to her house, she was already cut up pretty badly," Wright explained.

"Who?"

"Honey, it's Tina," Stone said.

"No, it can't be! She isn't in my address book!" Rissa cried.

"We believe that when he couldn't find you or the people in your book, he went for who he could find. She's still alive, Rissa. She's in ICU barely hanging on, but she's still alive."

"I have to see her! This is my fault!" Rissa cried.

"I'll take you to see her, but this isn't your fault. Do you understand me?" Stone knew no matter what he said she would blame herself.

"I won't hide anymore. If this is what happens when I hide—" She didn't finish the sentence. She was already out the door.

CHAPTER 4

"I BARELY KNEW HER WHEN Mom died, and now she's so important to me," Rissa whispered as she looked at Tina lying in the hospital bed.

"She loves you too." Chris, Tina's boyfriend, was sitting beside the hospital bed holding Tina's hand. "What's going on, Rissa?" Chris asked, looking at her. "Please, I have to know, and the police won't tell me anything since we aren't married," Chris said angrily. "They'll only tell me it has something to do with an ongoing investigation. And a cop guarding her hospital door scares me more than anything. A random attacker wouldn't come back to finish the job, so that tells me they think he might try again. *Why?*"

"This is my fault."

"How's that possible? You weren't even in town. Tina told me that you were taking some time off and…" His voice trailed off. "It was a cop that told her you were taking time off. What's going on? I don't understand."

Rissa took a ragged breath and told Chris everything. "There have been other attacks, and we don't know who's doing them or why. The cases are still open, and I promised I wouldn't discuss them. But I can't *not* tell you."

"Didn't you think you should have warned Tina?" Chris asked incredulously.

"Tina was never in my address book. I thought she'd be safe. I never imagined anyone would go after her, but I guess Stone thought of the possibility that she could be in danger because he put a man on her."

"A fat lot of good it did!" Chris's anger was palpable.

"The officer lost her in traffic. He tried to find her and then, realizing it was useless, went to her house. She arrived home before him," Rissa quietly explained in an agonized voice.

"Tina would have been careful if she had known she was in danger. She would've made sure not to lose her protection. She loves you, yet you didn't feel she was important enough to keep safe while you were hiding?" The anger in Chris's voice was sharp and the words stung. How could she not have warned Tina?

Stone had come up to the hospital room door during the conversation and had just listened. He promised Rissa some time, but he couldn't stand there and let Chris verbally attack her. He knew he'd be doing the same thing if the roles were reversed. But it was his fault, not Rissa's, that Tina hadn't been told.

Coming into the room, Stone said, "Rissa did everything we told her to do. We promised to keep her and those she was connected with as safe as possible. There was no way to know if Tina was a target. It was my decision not to tell Tina. I was afraid she would have panicked, and that wouldn't have helped anyone. I was wrong not to tell her; I'm sorry. I wish I could go back and change things." After a moment of tense silence Stone repeated, "I'm sorry." He turned and left the room.

Chris was holding Tina's hand, and Rissa was quietly crying. "I'm sorry I jumped all over you, but if I lose her..." Chris's voice was shaky, and tears were streaming down his face. Chris stared at Tina's hands in his. "She better be safe now!"

Rissa sat there a moment longer then went to find Stone.

STONE AND RISSA WERE BOTH doing a lot of thinking as they drove down the road. Stone wondered how he could make Rissa go back into hiding, and she was wondering how she could use herself as bait to lure this killer out. Neither would have liked what the other was thinking.

They reached Rissa's house, and since he entered before her, he was the first to see the destruction. Picture frames had been shattered, furniture had been ripped, walls had huge holes in them, curtains had been shredded, and that was just in the living room. Stone thought absently that he wouldn't have to sleep on that lumpy couch anymore. *What a stupid thing to be thinking about right now,* he berated himself.

He continued into the house, leaving Rissa standing in the entryway staring at the mess. The destruction didn't end with the front room. Every dish had been busted, food had been slung everywhere, the refrigerator doors had been left standing open, and several cabinet doors were ripped off the hinges. He went down the hall into the bathroom. Rissa's makeup had been crushed, the mirror was shattered, and everything that had been on her counters was now in the toilet.

The bedroom was the worst. Her mattress was ripped, her clothes were shredded, and her lamps were busted. There were more holes in the walls, and her dresser mirror had been shattered. The ceiling fan was lying in pieces on the bed. The carpet had something red smeared into it, and every personal item Rissa owned had been put in a pile and had the same red stuff poured over it.

Stone went back to find Rissa sitting on the floor of the entryway, rocking back and forth. "I just don't understand. Who hates me enough to hurt those I love and to do"—her arms swept wide—"this?"

Stone didn't have the answer but intended to get it. "I've called for the crime unit. I'm taking you somewhere safe then coming back here to see if they come up with anything."

Rissa didn't argue, which worried him even more than the destruction done to the house.

Stone took Rissa to his house. After showing her where things were, he left to go back to her home. She didn't know what to do with herself. She took a shower, trying unsuccessfully to wash off the guilt. She was wearing one of Stone's, way-too-big for her, t-shirts and a pair of his sweatpants. She had to roll the waistband down several times, and they were still gathered in a pool around her bare feet. She could smell Stone all around her, and it comforted her. She curled up in a ball on his massive bed and fell asleep.

That was how Stone found her a couple hours later. When he saw her on his bed and in his clothes his heart flipped. He walked over and sat on the edge of the bed, gently running his fingers through her hair. Her eyes slowly opened, and he could tell by the puffiness around her eyes that she had been crying and went to get some aspirin. He knew from having sisters that heavy crying caused a massive headache. Rissa watched him over the rim of the glass as she greedily took the aspirin he had given her.

"Thank you."

Giving her time to freshen up, he went to make sandwiches and coffee. He watched her closely as she came into the room, wondering how she was holding up. He knew he had to bring up the investigation but didn't want to. She did it for him.

"What'd you find out?" Her voice was quiet.

Stone sighed and sat down. "There are some confusing aspects to the damage done at your house."

"Such as?"

"Such as, most of the destruction seemed to be generalized, meaning not much thought went into it. It was done out of rage. We see this kind of rage in cases when someone wants revenge. The person wants to show them that they can't treat him this way, and he busts everything he can get his hands on."

"Okay, I think understand. It's usually a one-time thing fueled by a particular incident." Stone was impressed by how quickly she caught on. "What are the oddities? It looked like rage to me."

"Well, the oddities were in the bathroom and the bedroom. In the bathroom someone took the time to individually crush your makeup. In the bedroom, your clothes had been cut up. This indicates a more personal, pointed attack. There was thought put behind these things. I talked to Murphy, our profiler, and after a preliminary look he agreed. These acts were time consuming and meticulous. It was personal."

"And destroying my home isn't personal?"

"There are levels of rage. The damage to your personal items, items that you wear on your body, is consistent with a jealous lover. Such as if you were married or had a steady boyfriend and there was another woman or a woman who wanted you out of the picture so she could take your place. It has the feel of jealousy rather than rage."

"But that doesn't make sense since I'm single."

"That's where there's another oddity. Not a single picture of Matt was touched."

"I told you there is nothing between me and Matt."

"Yes, but when I saw the two of you together I doubted you. You also told me that most of his previous girlfriends didn't believe that."

"Why isn't Laura the target; they're engaged?"

"It could be one of his ex-girlfriends that blames you for her breakup with Matt. The thing is some of the damage done at your house would take considerable strength. Add that to the man's voice on the answering machine and the fact that it was a man you thought you saw at your work, and we're more confused than ever."

"Laura's been in his life for a long time now. Why would someone wait so long if it were a woman scorned?"

"We don't know. We don't even know if it has anything to do with an ex-girlfriend. Can you remember anyone who took it especially hard when Matt chose your relationship over theirs?" Stone asked.

"No one mad enough to kill!" Rissa was appalled at the thought that all of this could be happening because she and Matt were so close.

"It doesn't necessarily have to be anyone who threw a fit or was very outspoken. Jealousy is a strong motive, and sometimes the quiet ones are more dangerous than the outspoken ones."

"I don't know; you'd need to ask Matt. He's good looking and rich, very generous with his money, and he has a heart of gold. He lavishes gifts on his girlfriends and takes them on trips, and he is considered quite a catch. So as you can imagine, there have been a lot of girlfriends."

STONE TALKED TO MATT THAT evening while Rissa tried to sleep. She lay there, comforted by the deep resonance of his voice from down the hall. She couldn't believe she was falling in love with him during everything that was going on. No man other than Matt had been there for her, and no man, including Matt, had ever made her feel like Stone did.

She found that she liked the rugged cowboy look he had going on, and his five o'clock shadow accentuated the look. Dressed for work, he looked the part of the respectable detective, only he didn't wear the tie she thought most detectives would. But he was always dressed professionally when he was working. Then there were the times she had seen him dressed casually in jeans, and funny as it was for the city, he wore boots and a jean jacket during his time off. She guessed it was his Texas living during his youth. She had even found some flannel shirts in his closet when she had been looking for something to put on after her shower. She tried to imagine him in his youth on the ranch in Texas. She could picture him growing up there and becoming the sheriff of a Wild West town with a six gun on each hip, protecting the town from cattle barrens. He would fit the part perfectly with his tall, heroic demeanor, and she could picture all the saloon girls competing for his attention. Wow, she was never one for westerns, but apparently her mom's love of them had rubbed off. Rissa feel asleep thinking that her mom would have approved of Stone.

Rissa woke several hours later when Stone lay down beside her. He felt her tense up when he reached for her. "Honey, you're safe with me. I need to be near you and know that you are safe," Stone said in a low voice. He needed her as much as she needed him; the thought shocked her. She relaxed and let Stone hold her. It was for both of them, she realized. They both needed the connection.

"Was Matt helpful?" Rissa sleepily asked.

Stone chuckled, and she felt the rumble of his chest against her back. "Too much help. You were right; he has dated a lot! There's a lot of work going on at the station right now. I sent in the list Matt gave me. It'll take several days to locate all the women. But he gave us some interesting leads on a couple of them. They'll be the first to be checked out. Now go to sleep," he said as he gently kissed the tender spot at the curve of her neck and shoulder.

They laid in silence listening to the other breathe for so long that they each thought the other was asleep. "Good night, love," Stone whispered, pulling her even closer to him. Rissa smiled and went to sleep.

THE DAYS WERE EXCRUCIATINGLY SLOW when tracking down Matt's girlfriends took longer than expected. Some had married and some had moved out of state, and it took time to track those down. There were a couple that actually lived on other continents, and, while they weren't high on the list of suspects, their whereabouts had to be checked.

Most of the women had a lot to say about Rissa and Matt. Some of the stories had them secretly married, in love with each other but unwilling to admit it, and the most disturbing had them as brother and sister in love with each other. Everything had to be checked out, but that one was too ridiculous to even consider. There were bitter feelings toward Rissa by most of the women, but interestingly enough, the stories usually didn't involve Rissa being in them. The resentment was more from conversations they'd had with Matt. Several confirmed a statement Rissa had made days earlier about not having met some of the ladies, but that didn't stop the bitterness. Stone found that interesting. How could these women resent or even hate Rissa when they'd never met or spoken to her? But everyone appeared to have moved on.

"What's eating at you?" Wright asked.

"I don't know. We're missing something." There was something said or done that didn't fit. He knew it was important, but it remained elusive.

"Can you pin it down at all? Is it one of the women? The MO?" Wright knew enough to pay attention to Stone's gut. "We should receive the profile soon, and that might help."

"Speaking of the profile." A file was plopped on Stone's desk. "Hot off the presses and an interesting read. Look through it and call me when you're done. I'll come back down and answer any questions you might have."

"Thanks, Murphy." Stone dug into the file. Wright knew it would be a while before Stone resurfaced from the file and picked up the phone to order pizzas for everyone and charged them to Stone. He couldn't help but smile at the total. Stone would get even, of course, but that was half the fun. Wright was still trying to get that sexy lingerie shop to stop sending him e-mail alerts on sales and sending catalogs to his home. He had one heck of a time trying to explain to his wife why he bought over a hundred dollars of panties and was even more embarrassed when she made him return them. Once his wife realized that it was Stone who had ordered them and not her husband, she thought it was funny and it only encouraged Stone. Now Wright felt a little retribution was in order. No, Wright figured Stone was getting off easy with the $160 charge for pizzas.

What was left of the pizza was ice cold by the time Stone resurfaced. "Weird."

"What's weird?" Wright asked.

"Let's get Murphy back in here to go over this with us. Have him meet us in the war room. I'll be in there after I grab some pizza." Wright smiled as Stone picked up a slice of cold pizza and bit into it. Being a cop, you got used to eating when and what you could in the middle of a case.

They met in the war room, a stuffy room with a table surrounded by chairs. There were bulletin boards on three of the walls, and they were covered with crime scene photos. The fourth wall had a white board with a timeline. It also had pictures and notes on it and was constantly being updated as new information was received.

Murphy and the captain walked in, sat down, and waited for Stone to start. "I've looked over the profile, and it's unlike any I've ever seen. The standard stuff isn't there. There isn't anything to go on other than approximate age and race. Murphy…" Stone sat down and gave Murphy the lead.

"This is an unusual suspect, and that in itself says a lot. The perp shows male and female tendencies. The strength the perp demonstrates is confused with the instinctually female tendencies to go after the personal things. Men destruct out of rage, while women make things personal. Men will destroy makeup but it's because the makeup was dumped on the floor when the drawer was pulled out and then walked on because that's where it landed. But here the makeup was individually and meticulously crushed on the countertops. That takes time and has the personal touch women tend to possess. Same with the clothes—men throw them around, rip them, and sometimes defecate on them. But these were cut rather than torn. Couple that with the red nail polish poured over everything, and that indicates female tendencies."

"So what are we looking at?" asked Timmons, the rookie on the team.

"Well, if pushed, I would say you are looking at two perps."

The room erupted as everyone started talking at once. The captain watched Stone, who sat motionless, working things out in his head. The captain knew if anyone could crack the case, it would be Stone.

Stone stood, and everyone fell silent. "That's what has been bothering me. The calls were from a man, the strength is a man's, and the shadow was a man's. Men give flowers to women; women don't usually give each other roses. The man in the store buying the purse is connected; I feel it. He was too interested in what Rissa thought and what Rissa would want. But then there's the makeup and the clothes. Men don't think like that. If there are two people involved, then that opens the field considerably; gives us a lot of things to look at." Stone turned to Murphy. "Who's in charge? Who's leading who? One of them has to be instigating this. Once we can determine that, it'll help us know which way to go."

"I believe it's the woman," Murphy said.

"How does knowing that help?" Timmons asked again.

"If it's the man, we're looking for someone fixated on Rissa because of *his* feelings for her. If it's the woman, we're looking for someone who hates Rissa and is probably connected with Matt. Two different scenarios, two different investigative routes to take," Murphy said.

Stone thought for a moment. "I agree with Murphy. My gut's telling me the woman's the one pulling the strings. She's been hiding behind the man, staying in the shadows, while he's been the main focus. I think if we focus on the woman, our chances go up. Unless the male messes up, they won't get caught since he isn't directly connected except by the woman. We need to find the woman to solve this. Let's look at those women again. Only the ones cleared of the break-in will be taken off the list since that's the only time we can place the woman at the scene."

The captain stood up. "Let's get at it." The room emptied with a burst of noise as everyone was discussing the new turn of events.

CHAPTER 5

RISSA HAD BEEN SITTING BY Tina's side for several hours. She had finally talked Chris into going home to rest, eat, and shower. She'd been going over everything in her head and couldn't make sense of it. Who could hate her enough that they would want to hurt or kill those closest to her?

"How is she?"

Rissa jolted. "Oh, goodness, Laura. I was lost in my thoughts and didn't hear you come in."

Laura smiled, resting her hand on Rissa's shoulder. "Sorry. I wanted to come by and see you both. I know how close the two of you are. This must be awful for you."

"I haven't been able to come as often as I've wanted to. The store has been busy, and I can't close it down." Rissa sounded worn out.

"How about if I come in and help a couple hours a day this week?" She continued before Rissa could answer. "I wouldn't mind helping out, and it'll make Matt feel better to know that we're together. He's going out of his mind not being able to do more to help."

Rissa smiled. "Thank you. I could use some help. I know what you mean about Matt. He calls every couple of hours, and I think I've even seen him drive by the store several times in the last few days."

Laura looked startled for an instant. "I don't know why that surprises me. He's left to 'run errands,' and sometimes he doesn't even come back with anything." Laura laughed. "Now things make sense. I was starting to wonder if there was another woman."

Rissa was quick to defend Matt. "Of course there isn't! Matt loves you. You're good together."

"Oh, I know. I didn't really mean it. He's wonderful, and I don't ever plan to let him get away." Laura sounded distant as she talked. Then, seeming to snap out of it, she said, "Listen, I need to be going. What time do you need me tomorrow?"

"About ten for the midday rush would be great."

"Perfect! See you at ten." With that, Laura turned and left the room.

Rissa sat there for a moment with a frown creasing her forehead. "Strange," she muttered. She couldn't help but think that Laura was a little different today.

LAURA WAS TRUE TO HER word; she was there promptly at ten the next morning. *She is an attractive woman,* Rissa thought. Her makeup was always so meticulous that if Rissa hadn't seen her once without her makeup on, she would never have known that Laura had a smattering of freckles across her nose and cheeks. Laura was wearing a beautiful pumpkin-colored silk blouse that complemented rather than clashed with her strawberry blond hair. The heels she was wearing made her almost as tall as Rissa's five-foot-nine-inch height. Laura had a great figure, trim and toned.

Rissa really liked Laura's work ethics too. Laura worked four hours with enthusiasm and was open and friendly to everyone. She was chatty during down times, but Rissa still couldn't shake the feeling that something was off. Rissa made a mental note to talk to Matt and make sure everything was okay.

"So, Matt tells me you aren't staying at your house."

"No, but it's just temporary. I need to go home and get things cleaned up. Only being able to work on the mess when someone's there to keep on eye on me makes progress slow."

"I imagine it would make you a little crazy. I don't know how I'd handle it all. You're doing remarkably well."

Rissa gave a self-mocking and un-ladylike snort. "I'm not handling it that well. I cry a lot and have trouble sleeping. I snap at people for the littlest things. Stone and Matt both have commented that when this is over I need to take a vacation. I can't even think about that with this maniac still out there and Tina in a coma."

"Matt hates not knowing where you are. It makes him mad that neither you nor the detective will tell him where you're staying," Laura confided.

"After a long argument I promised Stone I wouldn't tell. Stone said someone could follow Matt when he came to see me. His argument was strengthened when Matt kept driving by, so I agreed to it temporarily. For now he has to be happy to see me at work or talk to me on my cell."

The chime over the door ended their conversation. Rissa stopped to watch Laura with the customer, thinking that Laura had as much reason to act strange as anyone else, with Matt's possible connection to the case. Rissa looked away just as Laura turned to look at her. The customer couldn't help but turn to look in the same direction. She was intrigued to see what had disgusted this nice lady so much that it was written all over her face. But the customer didn't see anything out of the ordinary, only the lady behind the counter.

"COME ON, STONE; TELL ME where she's staying. I can't take not knowing where she is and how she's doing." Matt ran his fingers through his hair, a habit Stone had noticed Matt had when he was frustrated.

"I understand, but Rissa's safety comes first." Stone's impression of Matt had changed over the last few days, and it wasn't a good change.

"I would never let any harm come to Rissa."

"You and I both know that you won't be able to help yourself. You're in the daily report as having driven by her work no less than six times a day. The officer wanted to bring you in for questioning." Stone gave Matt a withering look. "He was so interested in you that he might have neglected noticing a real suspect." Or had the officer's instincts been right on, Stone wondered.

Matt looked chagrined. "I need to make sure she's okay!"

"That's my point." Stone sighed and added, "Look, she has her cell, so you can call her anytime, and you can see her at work now that the officer won't haul you in, shackled in handcuffs."

Matt looked unhappy but relented. "All right, I get it, but it doesn't make it easier. I need to do more."

"Then let's get back to this list of names. There were more women than I had expected that hate Rissa, and most of them had little or no contact with her. It seems when you tire of a woman you start comparing her to Rissa. They haven't seemed to appreciate that."

Wright added under his breath. "I can't imagine why."

Stone continued. "I see a pattern that you use Rissa to get out of relationships. I don't think Rissa even knows you do it. You compare the women often enough that they leave you, blaming Rissa, when the whole time it's you using her." The root of Stone's new insight into Matt made it hard for him to continue, but Stone didn't want Matt to know he was now a suspect. What he really wanted to do was wring Matt's neck, and it took every ounce of his willpower not to tip his hand. It irked him to have to play up to Matt to get him to open up, but he knew from experience that if you intimidated a suspect at the wrong time, he would clam up.

"I know you love Rissa and don't mean to use her. I don't know if you realize what you're doing to her in the eyes of these women. I bet given the chance, Rissa could have been friends with them, like she and Laura are. You and Rissa are close, and some of the women might not have been able to handle that, but I bet most of them would have."

Matt was going to argue. Stone could see it in his eyes and the way his back stiffened. Part of Stone wished he would deny it. Stone really wanted to come down hard on Matt, but the only thing that betrayed his thoughts was the look of barely suppressed rage in his eyes. Matt opened his mouth to deny the accusations, but one look at Stone and Matt swallowed hard and looked away. He stared at the worn, cracked linoleum, shaking his head. Stone could tell Matt was having an internal debate with himself. He absently wondered who would win the debate: the devil on Matt's left shoulder or the angel on his right shoulder. Stone realized the angel had won when Matt finally started talking.

"This is my fault; I didn't realize...It was easier if they broke things off. I figured if they left me they would feel better about the breakup. I never thought about the effect my actions had on Rissa." Matt's voice broke. "I would never hurt Rissa. If I had known...I wouldn't have ever...tell me this isn't because of me. I love Rissa. She is the only family I have. Oh man, this can't be happening." Matt's outpouring did nothing to improve Stone's impression of him. In Stone's mind, there was little to nothing Matt could do to redeem himself.

"When I heard what these women had to say I wanted to beat you to a bloody pulp. What you've done is not only disgraceful, but because of what you've set in motion due to your own cowardice, she is blaming herself for everything that's happened. In the time I've known her she has lost weight, can't sleep, and jumps down your throat with little or no provocation. What you've done to her is cold. You never once considered Rissa in the love 'em and leave 'em game you've been playing."

Matt was openly crying now. Stone had a death grip on the edge of the desk, afraid of what he would do if he got his hands on Matt. The regret was etched on Matt's face, but that did little to change Stone's opinion of Matt. Something would have to change. Stone wanted to remain in Rissa's life but knew he'd never be able to stand by and let Matt use her. Stone took a steadying breath, knowing his anger wouldn't help anything right now.

"Help fix this. I asked you to go over the original list and make sure you didn't forget anyone. Did you get it done?"

Matt wiped his eyes and scooted his chair closer to the table. "I went back over the list, and other than one-night stands, Laura is the only other woman I've dated."

"Okay, we haven't looked at Laura because she doesn't fit the profile, but we will," Stone stated.

"Laura would never do this. She and Rissa are friends," Matt rebuffed.

"I think it's a waste of time too," Wright added. "Matt never compared Laura to Rissa, and Matt and Laura are still together."

Matt cleared his throat, and both detectives looked at him. "I don't think I'm going to like what you have to tell me, am I?" Stone asked Matt in a low, flat, and deceptively quiet tone. Wright knew that tone, and it meant trouble.

"Laura isn't like anyone else I've ever dated. She mesmerized me from the beginning, and that scared me spitless. I tried to push her away by doing what I always did. Laura cried, screamed, and threw things, but she held tough. We worked through it, and I realized Laura was the best thing that ever happened to me. We have a good relationship, and Laura and Rissa have become friends." Matt refused to look at Stone, and he was man enough to admit that he was more than a little afraid of him.

Stone was coiled to strike, and Wright knew it. "Stone, why don't you check on Rissa while Matt and I go through the names left on the list? Then you can start the background check on Laura." Wright was trying to diffuse the situation; even through his rage at Matt, Stone recognized that. Stone stood up hard, causing his chair to make a loud noise and almost fall over, making Matt look up. The look on Stone's face made it clear that if anything happened to Rissa, Matt couldn't run far enough or fast enough.

Matt turned to Wright as Stone walked out. "Thanks. I think he would have come over the table for me."

Wright looked at him with disgust. "I didn't do it for you."

IN THE MEN'S ROOM, STONE splashed cold water on his face, trying to get himself under control. He looked at his reflection in the mirror and grimaced at the look on his face. Needing to hear Rissa's voice, he turned abruptly and headed for his desk to call her.

"Hey." Rissa's warm greeting helped dampen Stone's cold rage.

"I wanted to make sure everything's okay," Stone said lamely. It wasn't what he wanted to say, but until this was all over, it was all he could say.

"Things are quiet now, but it's been busy." He could hear the exhaustion in her voice. "Are you picking me up, or should I ride with Jenkins?"

"Well, *Jenkins* shouldn't be anywhere near you for you to know his name, and he isn't supposed to be your chauffeur, but your protection." Stone's voice had Rissa's ears picking up trouble for Officer Jenkins.

"Look, he didn't do anything wrong. I needed a break and went outside. I noticed him down the street, and I approached him. I tried to talk him into coming inside, but he stayed professional and refused. Don't get on to him," Rissa defended the officer.

Stone took a deep breath, letting it out slowly. "I'll be there to pick you up, and Jenkins is safe this time. Sorry, it's been a rough day. I'll be there soon." They said their good-byes and hung up.

AT CLOSING TIME, RISSA CAME out as Stone pulled into the parking lot. He couldn't help but smile at the sight of her. Getting in the truck, she turned to say hi only to be kissed instead.

"I needed that. It's been a really trying day," Stone said in a tired voice, emphasizing how trying the day actually had been.

"My pleasure, glad I could help." Rissa said as Stone leaned over and kissed her again.

From his squad car, Officer Jenkins smiled; now he knew why Stone was so protective. Jenkins pulled out into the flow of traffic, not noticing the car two spots behind him. The driver had also been watching the interaction between Stone and Rissa, but the driver wasn't smiling. The car pulled into the flow of traffic a few car lengths behind Stone's truck, careful not to get too close.

Stone was watching an older model blue Towne Car behind them. Pulling into a drive-thru for dinner, he watched to see if the car would follow them, but it didn't even slow down as it drove past. Stone relaxed a little and didn't notice when a burgundy jeep pulled in behind them as they left the parking lot, headed toward his home. As he got close to his street, traffic had thinned and he finally noticed the unfamiliar jeep. The area he lived in was an older, established neighborhood. He knew most of the cars that were commonly seen in the area, and the jeep wasn't one of them. When it turned two streets before he did, he relaxed and pushed the jeep out of his mind. It wasn't as if he knew every car in the area.

Stone and Rissa were in the house eating dinner and going over their day, unaware of the Towne Car and the jeep driving up and down the residential streets looking for Stone's truck. The driver of the jeep finally called the driver of the Towne Car, relaying the address of Detective Stone's house, then drove away.

STONE DEBATED ALL NIGHT ON whether to say anything to Rissa about Matt. In the end he decided against telling Rissa anything about what Matt had done. With everything else going on she didn't need to deal with Matt's betrayal. Stone knew that one way or another Matt would tell her about what he had done. If Stone knew Rissa, she would be hurt, even mad, but she'd forgive him. It aggravated Stone to know that she would forgive Matt when he was the cause of all of this misery, but that was part of the reason he was so drawn to her. She was genuinely a good person. He'd seen so much hate and indifference in his line of work that it was refreshing to meet someone like her. Stone shook his head and got back to work.

It was barely November, and the temperature was getting colder; so was the case. It was hard to believe that Rissa had only been in his life for such a short amount of time. It seemed as though he had known her forever, yet not long enough. In a case like this, it wasn't unusual for it to go on for months, even years, but Stone wanted it to end as soon as possible. He didn't want Rissa in danger, and he had things he wanted to say to her that he couldn't let himself say as long as the case was still open. He needed to stay focused; he would never forgive himself if something happened to Rissa because he was distracted.

Nothing had happened in the two weeks since Tina had been attacked and Rissa's house had been ransacked. The calls had stopped, but that was because she wasn't staying at home anymore. If she was being watched, the stalker would know that. But was she still being watched? Stone took her to his house every night and hadn't seen anyone suspicious following them. That would be too obvious anyway. Maybe the stalker was smart enough to realize he would get caught if he followed them. Maybe he was willing to watch her from a distance and bide his time. Stone slammed his fist on the desk. It just didn't feel right, to go from killing and constantly harassing and terrorizing Rissa to nothing. Something had changed, but what?

He was sitting at his desk going over his notes when his phone rang. "Detective Stone," he answered.

"Detective, this is Trudy Scotts. I had a message to call you."

"Yes, thank you for returning my call. I'm trying to reach everyone connected to an investigation I'm conducting. Your daughter, Laura's, name has come up as a possible witness." He never used the word *suspect* because it put people on the defensive.

"What is it you need? Why don't you just ask Laura?"

Laura hadn't been any help at all when he and Wright had talked to her. All Laura would say was that she couldn't imagine why anyone would want to hurt Rissa. But when questioned about her past, she would only say it was too painful to talk about.

"Can you tell me about some of Laura's past boyfriends?" Stone was trying to ease her into talking about family, which was never easy. "Or about any problems she may have had with any woman over a man they might have both been attracted to?" Stone was hoping to find a pattern in behaviors toward anyone who might have been a rival for a man's affection. It was the same line of questioning he had used with the other women on Matt's list, but it was always easier when talking to the actual suspect. They were usually more willing to talk than a family member might be. Stone knew from experience that a mom was a hard nut to crack and usually clammed up when questioned about a child, but he didn't need to worry about this mom; she didn't seem to have the same family loyalties that most parents did.

"Laura didn't date. She was a loner during school and kept to herself for the most part."

"What about more recently? Say, in the last five years. How have her relationships been?"

"I can't help you; I haven't seen Laura in years. What is this all about? I thought you said she was a witness; it sounds like you are investigating her."

So maybe there was a little family loyalty. "Why haven't you seen her in years, Mrs. Scotts?" Stone queried, ignoring the woman's question.

Mrs. Scotts seem to balk at answering the question for a moment and then sighed heavily. "We never had money, and it embarrassed her. Once she was old enough to leave home, she didn't hesitate. She went to make a better life for herself."

"Do you ever hear from her?" Stone wasn't sure, but Mrs. Scott's speech sounded slurred. Since it was just before lunch, Stone wondered how early Mrs. Scotts hit the bottle.

"No. She blames me for our life. Said I never tried to better our situation. She's prob'ly right. Trailer parks never bothered me, but it was never good 'nuff for Laura." Mrs. Scotts sounded as if she cared less.

"Do you know anyone who might still be in contact with her?" Stone figured it was worth a shot.

"She never had friends that I could tell, but she and her little brother stayed close. She always doted on that boy."

"Do you know where I can find him?"

"Not 'xactly. I haven't seen hide nor hair of him for a couple of years; he just took off one day."

Stone could tell he was starting to lose Mrs. Scotts. "Ma'am, what's your son's name?"

"Billy." With that, she hung up.

Stone conveyed the conversation he'd just had with Laura's mom to Wright.

"So Laura isn't close to her mom and brother. I can see why from your impressions of the mom. But I don't see anything that would point the finger at Laura for the harassment. We need to talk to the brother and see what he has to say."

Stone agreed, but as he finished his notes about the conversation, something bothered him. Mrs. Scotts was a piece of work, and Stone couldn't blame Laura for wanting to better her life, but the scenario Mrs. Scotts had painted of her daughter didn't quite jive with the impression he'd gotten of Laura. There was something that just didn't sit right about the conversation, and as he was reaching for the phone to call Matt, it rang.

"Detective Stone," he answered. After listening to what the caller had to say, he swore under his breath. "I'll be right there." He hung up, grabbed his jacket, and motioned for Wright to follow.

"OH, MAN!" WRIGHT SAID, LOOKING around Stone's ransacked house. From the outside, everything looked normal. If a neighbor looking for his pet hadn't seen the back door open and called it in, Stone wouldn't have known about it until he brought Rissa home tonight.

The damage wasn't as bad as at Rissa's place. The destruction was mild when you compared the two, but there were enough similarities to know it was the same person. The crime scene investigators were there collecting evidence, so Stone, Wright, Murphy, and the captain all leaned against the side of Stone's truck and let them work. Stone mentioned his impressions of the scene.

"From the short time I was in there, I agree. It's the same people, but the hate they have for Rissa isn't conveyed in what they did here. I think this was more of a 'we know where you are' type of thing. It's designed to scare her and keep her from feeling safe," Murphy said.

Stone hit the side of his truck. "I knew I was being followed last night. I should have listened to my gut."

"No use with the 'should haves,'" Captain said. "Where's Rissa now?"

"At work; Jenkins is on watch," Wright answered.

"Call and tell him to be on alert; these people are tired of waiting. They're becoming bolder. Ransacking a high-ranking detective's home in broad daylight isn't subtle." Captain turned to Stone. "You need to find another place to keep her."

"I know." After a moment of watching the activity around his home he took out his cell phone to call Rissa.

"Hey, I didn't expect you to be calling this time of day," Rissa said, pleasantly surprised.

"I wanted to check in and make sure you are okay."

"Sure. Laura and I are winding down from the midday rush. She's been a huge help."

"Has anything out of the ordinary happened today?"

"No, it's been a normal day." Rissa was starting to feel uneasy. "What's going on?"

Stone hedged for a moment then finally said, "My house was ransacked."

"I don't know what to say. I feel…numb. Stone, I'm sorry. I seem to be a curse to anyone around me."

Stone silently cursed Matt again. "Honey, it isn't your fault." The captain's eyebrows shot up at Stone's use of the endearment. "We'll find this person, and that's a promise." One he should never make but knew he would do everything to keep.

Laura was right there when Rissa hung up. "What's wrong?"

"Someone ransacked Stone's house."

"I bet they were letting you know you weren't safe staying there any longer."

"I don't know what to do."

"Why don't you go out to the country house for a while? Matt will rest easier knowing where you are, and you will be safe there. I'll come out and stay for a few days, until I have to get back to work. The symphony is gearing up for holiday concerts, and our pre-holiday rest is about over. But since it's Thursday and I don't have to be back until Monday, I can spare a long weekend." When Rissa didn't seem convinced Laura added, "I've moved some of my stuff out to Matt's so I don't have so much to move after the wedding, and I would love your company while I'm getting things unpacked and put away."

"I don't want to put you two in danger."

Laura shook her head. "You know that if anything happened to you, Matt would never get over it. No one knows about Matt's place; you'll be safe there. Call Matt and talk to him." Laura dialed Matt's number and handed the phone to Rissa.

CHAPTER 6

"COME ON, RISSA TOLD ME about your place. No matter what you think of me, you know I'd never let anything happen to her. She'll be safe out here, and we can keep it quiet for as long as possible. She doesn't want to hide, but we need to convince her to come out here. She didn't even want to call me, but Laura was there when you called Rissa, and she made Rissa call me."

Stone knew Matt was right. It was the only thing he'd come up with too. Stone knew something was about to happen, and he didn't want Rissa around when it did. It took a lot of convincing to get Rissa to agree. Stone had a plan that hopefully would end all of this, and it wouldn't work if she were in town.

"What is it?" Rissa demanded when Stone tried to convince her to go into hiding again.

"We want to put an undercover policewoman in your place and let everyone know that you're taking time off to get your house in order. Hopefully we'll lure the killer out into the open. We'll have officers stationed nearby, listening to everything going on in your house, ready to spring the trap." Rissa had only agreed because she knew they could put her in protective custody, and she didn't want that.

"I feel horrible running every time something happens." Rissa held up her hand before Stone could argue. "But if we can end all this, then I'll do as you ask. But if this doesn't work, I won't hide or run away again."

Stone heaved a sigh of relief, pulling Rissa into his arms. "I need to hold you. When this is over I'd like the chance to get to know you. I want to know if you like bowling, fishing, hiking, canoeing, or camping. I want to know what it's like to end a date with a kiss at the door rather than a gun drawn, checking closets and under beds." Rissa gave a shaky laugh. "I want to know what it is like to say 'I love you' for the first time and to hear you say you love me." Stone closed his eyes, hoping he hadn't said too much.

Rissa pulled back to look at him; the worry in his eyes had her smiling. "I can tell you one thing; you don't have to wait. I love you. I have for some time now. I was afraid I would blurt it out when I wasn't ready, but if I don't make it through this I want you to know I love you. I love to hear your voice, and I love that you can hold me at night, lying in the same bed, and not try to take it any further. I love that you recognize that I'm not prepared for that next step.

Call me old fashioned, but I always believed that love and marriage come first." Rissa hadn't intended to mention marriage, but sex before marriage wasn't in her agenda. She had made a promise to herself and her mom, and she intended to keep it.

"Rissa, I haven't always done what's right, and I've regretted some choices I've made, but one thing's for sure: I admire you and your beliefs, and more importantly, I respect them. I don't have any problem waiting until our wedding night to be with you."

Tears ran down Rissa's face. She had been ridiculed many times because she wouldn't put out. "My mom told me the right one would come along and would understand. I guess she was right."

"Are you okay knowing I have a past?"

Rissa laughed. "I can't imagine you being anyone other than who you are, and that means accepting the whole package."

"I love you, Rissa," Stone said then gently kissed her. "Will you go out with me when this is over?"

The reminder of their situation came crashing back, but she smiled up at him and said, "I'd love to."

ONCE RISSA AGREED WITH STONE'S plan, things happened fast. Stone didn't want Rissa in town for one more night. He got everything set up while Rissa packed a bag. They rode in silence to the same parking garage as before. Stone parked beside an almost new Mustang with heavily tinted windows. Rissa looked at Stone with a questioning glance.

"I wanted you to have something fast in case you needed it." He didn't say in case of what; he didn't need to.

The woman who got out of the Mustang had Rissa taking a second look. "Wow, she looks enough like me to be my sister."

"She doesn't hold a candle to you." Stone wiped a tear off Rissa's cheek as she turned away from her doppelganger. "We'll get this guy, I promise."

"You be careful. I don't want to lose you just when I've found you." Stone gave her a kiss full of promises to come.

Getting back to the matter at hand, Stone said, "When you leave, don't go directly to Matt's house. Drive around, making frequent turns. A silver Buick LeSabre will follow you to make sure no one's tailing you. It'll be Jenkins. I figured you would feel more comfortable with him. Once he calls and gives the all clear, head on out to Matt's. Do you have any questions?"

Rissa shook her head. "I just want this to be over." With that, she slid out of the truck and got in the Mustang. She watched her look-alike get in the truck and sit beside Stone exactly as she had. Crying, Rissa drove away, doing exactly what Stone had told her to do.

The female officer had jumped at the chance to work this case. Everyone wanted a chance to work with Stone; he was a legend in the making. The fact that he was unattached and extremely handsome didn't hurt. But after witnessing the exchange at the garage she knew he was off limits. That, mixed with the intensity coming from him, left no room for friendly conversation. Stone had his arm around her shoulder, but there was no warmth in the touch; it was for show.

The next morning, when Stone called to ask Matt to come in, he agreed, but there was an edge to his voice. He almost seemed scared and resentful of Stone. Rissa didn't understand what was going on but didn't have the opportunity to ask Matt any questions.

"I know you want to come home, but nothing's happened yet," Stone said when Rissa got on the phone. "I feel it Rissa, something's going to happen soon. I want you home and close to me but for now I need to know you're safe. I love you." Rissa kept replaying those words in her head all morning.

It seemed that, other than Stone's house being ransacked, the stalker had stopped. Would the killer believe the cops would leave her unattended at her house? Rissa doubted it.

The day dragged on, and Laura was always close by; the combination was wearing on Rissa's nerves. She couldn't go anywhere that Laura didn't find some excuse to be in the same room. The only place Rissa could find solitude was the bathroom. She had only been in the bathroom a couple of minutes when she was startled by a knock. "Yes?"

"Are you okay?"

Rissa took a calming breath. "I'm going to take a quick shower. Be out in a bit." When she came out of the bathroom thirty minutes later she saw Laura hurrying into Matt's room. Had she been watching for her to come out? Why? Rissa told herself she was being ridiculous. She stuck her head in Matt's room and noticed the smell. "Is that lilacs?"

Laura turned sharply, startled. "Yes, I liked the perfume from your store, so I bought a bottle."

"It's my favorite scent." Rissa changed subjects. "I need to get out for a bit. I'm going to walk around the property."

"Are you sure you should? Maybe I should go with you."

"*No,*" Rissa said more forcibly than she meant to. "No," she repeated, softening her tone. "I need some space. I promise I won't go far."

Laura looked as though she wanted to object, but Rissa was supposed to be safe out here. No one knew she was here; no one even knew about this place. Before Laura could find an excuse to go with her, Rissa grabbed her coat and hurried outside.

"I TOLD YOU I CAN'T think of anyone else. Laura and I have been together a year," Matt repeated. Everyone in the room looked aggravated. They had been going at it all day, and everyone was tired and hungry.

"Are there any leads not tied down yet?" Captain asked.

"No, the women either have alibis or no motive. All calls have been returned, or we've found them following a different avenue. The only call we still have out is on Laura's brother," Stone said.

"Laura's an only child," Matt corrected.

"No, she has a younger brother, Billy."

"She doesn't have a brother," Matt said.

"I got this information from her mom, and I confirmed it in the database. Trudy Scotts, divorced with two children: a daughter, Laura Scotts, and a son, William Owens; they're actually half siblings. Billy is twelve years younger than Laura. His dad, Charles Owens, was drunk and fell while climbing a ladder, crushing his skull. Billy was eight. Laura's father is unknown, and her mom never re-married. We probably wouldn't have known about her brother without Mrs. Scotts' help since he has a different last name," Stone read from his notes.

"That can't be. She said she was an only child." Matt shook his head in puzzlement.

"What else has Laura told you?" Stone asked.

Old Acquaintances

AS RISSA WALKED BACK TOWARD the house, she could see Laura standing at the window. *Is she watching me?* Rissa wondered. She sighed and felt the sting of frustrated tears, wishing she didn't have to go back, wishing she could go home, wishing Stone would come get her and tell her everything was okay.

When she got back to the house she didn't see Laura anywhere. But there was a cup of hot tea on the counter with some cookies and a note: "Help yourself. I'll be in my room. Let me know when you'd like some company."

Laura was trying to be nice, and Rissa was being ungrateful. Feeling guilty, Rissa took a sip of the tea; it had a bitter taste that she found distasteful. She took a couple more sips so she wouldn't offend Laura. Rissa suddenly felt hot all over, and while setting the teacup down, she spilled most of it on the counter and in the plate of cookies. Not wanting Laura to see that she had ruined her thoughtful gesture, Rissa quickly cleaned it up. She was just finishing when she heard Laura coming down the hall. Rissa turned around to thank Laura when her head starting spinning and she could feel her pulse pounding in her head; the combination was disorienting.

"Are you okay?" Laura asked, her voice sounding far away.

"I'm a little lightheaded and my head hurts," Rissa said in a weak voice.

Laura helped Rissa sit down at the table. "Let me get you some aspirin. I have some in my purse. Just a sec."

Rissa couldn't understand why the room was spinning. She was still sitting there when Laura returned. "I know I have some in here," Laura said, rummaging through her purse.

Rissa couldn't take her eyes off the pretty beaded purse. It looked identical to one Rissa had sold some time back. But that couldn't be; she bought those purses from a woman who handmade them, and she promised she never duplicated her work.

"Your purse..." Rissa managed to say.

"It's lovely, isn't it? It was a gift from my brother; he went to a great deal of risk to buy it for me. It wasn't safe, but he was doing something nice for me, so what could I do?" Laura was almost bubbly.

Rissa couldn't seem to focus and laid her head down. She wasn't sure how long she had been like that, but she was startled to realize that there were two different voices in the next room. She started to call out, thinking Matt or Stone had come back, but something made her stop.

That voice. The voice talking to Laura. It was the same one on her answering machine. But that couldn't be right; she must be wrong. *I need to warn Laura,* Rissa thought, yet her instincts told her to hold still.

"You're sure you gave me enough to keep her out?" Laura's voice was suddenly closer.

"I'm sure. If you gave her all of it, she won't wake up for hours," the man said.

"Good. We'll have to set the house up to look like her stalker followed her here and killed her. I'll be the sole survivor, crying my eyes out about how I tried to help her and got cut in the process. I'll be the hero, and she'll be out of our lives forever." Laura sounded giddy. Rissa could tell that they were leaving the kitchen when she suddenly sneezed. Her head was forcibly lifted off the table by her hair, and she screamed.

"So, you're awake." Rissa could hear hair being ripped out of her head. "Billy, get the rope. We'll tie her up then start on the house."

Billy disappeared while Laura continued to hold Rissa's head back at a painful angle. Billy returned and tied Rissa to the chair. When he was close enough that Rissa's eyes could focus on his face, she recognized him as the man from the shop who had bought the purse and lilac perfume. The one she could barely understand because he mumbled. Once she was tied up, Laura let go of Rissa's hair.

"Billy, get started." Laura turned her back to Billy and sat across the table from Rissa. "Why aren't you still out? There were enough drugs in that tea to put two people your size down."

"I spilled some of it," Rissa slurred. "It's been you all along?" A buried memory of Laura mentioning that Stone's house was ransacked to let her know she wasn't safe anymore came back to her. Laura couldn't have known that she was staying at Stone's house. How stupid could she have been not to have seen that then?

"Oh yes, Billy and me," Laura bragged. "You see, I got tired of Matt comparing me to you. I threw quite the fit, and Matt finally realized I was perfect for him. But no matter what I did, it was always you he called when he needed to talk. He was always running to you when you needed him. It was always you and will always be you, and I can't have that."

Rissa was confused. "What are you talking about? He would never compare us. He loves you!"

"Yes, he loves me, but he loves you more. Maybe not in the same way, but still…" Laura got up and paced the room. She spun suddenly with fury in her eyes, spittle spraying when she spoke. "I've worked too long and hard to find a man like Matt: rich, single, and no family. I won't let someone as insignificant as you destroy everything! Don't you see? Matt's perfect. I need money to live the kind of life I was always meant to live. With me on his arm guiding him to be prosperous in the social circles, we'll be the most admired couple around. Everyone will want us at their parties and their grand openings. I'll be on the cover of social magazines." Laura had gone crazy.

That's all there was to it. Laura was certifiable. *And she's going to kill me,* Rissa thought.

"But those things aren't Matt."

"*They will be!*" Laura screamed then stopped herself and straightened up, visibly pulling herself together. "He will either become the type, or he'll be taken out of the picture. I'll become the loving, grieving widow. Either way, it works for me!" Laura gave a little giggle, and fear raced down Rissa's spine. Rissa prayed for a miracle.

MATT CLUNG TO THE HANDLE above the passenger door. He couldn't believe Laura was behind all of this. The pieces were coming together, only, they hoped, not too late for Rissa. The background check on Laura and Billy finally came back. Laura had been a person of interest in Billy's dad's death, but it was eventually ruled an accident. The officer that worked the case never believed it, though.

Laura took off when she was seventeen. Billy left home at eighteen; their mom hadn't seen either of them since. Billy dropped off the radar, and Laura had kept a low profile until she started at the college symphony.

Stone hadn't said much once Matt told him it had been Laura who told him to get Rissa home from her vacation because he was driving her nuts. And it was Laura's idea that Rissa stay at the country house. Laura had insisted that only she and Matt cared enough about her to keep her safe.

Stone's truck was going at speeds that Matt thought they only put on the speedometer to impress. He didn't know the needle would actually go that high, and he hoped he never had to find out again. Stone hadn't spoken since he'd realized that he'd all but hand delivered Rissa to her stalker.

Watching Stone, Matt almost felt sorry for Laura. Almost. He spent the rest of the drive praying for Rissa and that he and Stone wouldn't be too late.

STONE COULDN'T BELIEVE HE HADN'T figured it out sooner. If Rissa died, he wouldn't be able to live with himself. He promised to protect and serve, and he couldn't protect the one person who had come to mean more to him than anyone else. Not only that, but he had made it easy for Laura!

Stone had the speedometer at top speed, and it felt like he was in mud. It was normally an hour drive, but Stone estimated it would be closer to twenty minutes. He'd tried to call Rissa to warn her, but no one was answering the home phone or her cell phone. After trying unsuccessfully to warn Rissa, knowing Matt had his own cell phone, he'd told Matt to continue trying to reach her. Stone called the sheriff's department to get them to send someone out to the country house. The sheriff's department was sending someone immediately, but at the speed Stone was going, Stone was likely to get there before anyone else. Stone wasn't taking any chances that the sheriff's department would feel the same sense of urgency he did or be willing to risk their own lives to get there as fast as possible, so Stone had the accelerator all the way to the floor.

Laura should have been at the top of the suspect list once Matt's involvement was uncovered, but Stone allowed his personal feelings to cloud his judgment. He should have checked her out instead of relying on character accounts from Matt and Rissa.

For the most part, Laura had stayed with the truth, but the lies she told were coming unraveled now. Laura didn't want anyone to know she had a brother because he was her little secret. He had done all her dirty work, leaving Laura in the clear. Until recently, Laura hadn't actually been involved directly with the threat to Rissa. But they found out she hadn't gone with the symphony several times she said she had. She had stayed behind to help follow Rissa when her brother would be noticed if he were always around. She had lied about the symphony being on break so she could volunteer to help at the store to keep tabs on Rissa and to try to find out what the cops knew. She had told the college that she had to take a short leave due to a family emergency. Stone should have known the symphony wouldn't take a break just before all the holiday concerts coming up. How stupid he had been. He was so focused on the case and not on the most obvious suspect that the one lie that should have tripped her up immediately went unnoticed. Being on break from the symphony also made it possible for her to help with the break-ins, at least the one at Rissa's.

Stone couldn't lose Rissa. He had finally found the person he wanted to grow old with. Stone had never prayed so hard in his life.

MATT OPENED HIS EYES WHEN the truck slowed down. Having been unable to reach anyone at the house, he had been doing a lot of praying. He realized the headlights were off when he had trouble seeing. Stone stopped the truck at the road leading to the country house, did something to the overhead light, then checked his gun.

"Stay out of my way!" Stone growled as he got out, and Matt realized that he'd fixed the overhead light so it wouldn't come on. Matt got out and stayed ten feet behind Stone as he raced up the driveway.

"BILLY, ARE YOU DONE YET?" Laura yelled, never taking her eyes off Rissa.

"Almost," Billy answered from somewhere in the house.

"You don't have to do this! He loves you," Rissa pleaded.

Laura smiled. "Yes, but I won't share him. He will be mine and mine alone, or no one will have him."

There was a crash in the other room.

"Billy? What are you doing?" Silence answered her. "*Billy!*" Laura yelled.

The lights went out. Laura screamed, and Rissa jerked her chair over so that she was lying on the floor. She didn't know what was going on, but she didn't want Laura to have an exact fix on her. Rissa had been working on her ropes while Laura had been talking; they were loose, but not enough.

"Rissa?" Laura whispered. "Billy?" Laura called quietly as she left the room.

The house was pitch black. Rissa didn't know if Stone had arrived or if the lights went out due to some freaky coincidence. But she was going in favor of Stone's gut and decided not to believe in coincidence. As Rissa managed to get the ropes off, she heard screaming and gun shots. The darkness was the worst part of it because she didn't know what was going on. The silence that followed was so absolute that it made her ears ring. She held still, not wanting Laura or Billy to find her. She heard shuffling footsteps coming into the kitchen.

"I can't see anything! Turn the lights back on!"

Rissa heard Stone yell from the other room. She knew that whoever was in the kitchen with her wasn't Stone. When the lights came back on, she was looking at Laura's back. Rissa was in the opposite corner from where she had been tied up. Almost in slow motion, Laura, holding a small pistol, turned to where Rissa was hiding. Laura was bleeding from her chest and was gurgling blood. Rissa knew Laura didn't have much time, but also didn't want to die with her.

Rissa saw a flurry of movement from the corner of her eye, heard a gunshot, and screamed all at the same time. With the smell of cordite still in the air, Rissa opened her eyes, realizing she didn't hurt anywhere, at least not until she saw Matt lying lifeless and bleeding directly in front of her. Then she felt more pain than she had in her entire life.

"Matt!" Rissa cried. "Matt, don't do this to me. I can't lose you too! Oh, Mattie, please." Rissa was pressing on the wound in Matt's chest, tears streaming down her face. Rissa spared a glance at Laura and knew by her glazed eyes that she was dead.

Stone came in, gun drawn, and took in the scene in an instant. He went to Laura, checking for a pulse, then ran to Matt to try to control the bleeding. Rissa couldn't do anything but cry and hold Matt's hand, telling him to hang on as sirens could be heard closing in on the house.

CHAPTER 7

IT TOOK SEVERAL DAYS TO wrap everything up. With what Laura had told Rissa and what Stone already knew, most of their questions were answered and they just had to accept there would be some questions never answered. Laura couldn't bear the thought of sharing Matt, so she enlisted the help of her brother and decided to terrorize and ultimately kill Rissa. Billy was in jail and had sung like a bird.

Stone hadn't seen much of Rissa in the last couple of days; she went back and forth between Matt's and Tina's hospital rooms. Matt had been in critical condition for the first two days, but on the third day he had been downgraded to intensive. As long as he didn't get an infection, he should pull through.

Tina finally came out of her coma. She was able to identify Billy as her attacker, not that the identification was necessary since Billy had confessed to everything. Rissa told Tina everything, the whole time fearing Tina would hate her, but Tina never once blamed Rissa.

When Tina was awake and out of danger, Rissa never left Matt's room. She was there when he finally woke up. She kissed his face all over and cried. He was in terrible pain, but he needed to feel her and know she was okay.

Once the nurse came in and gave him some morphine, he was up to talking. He told Rissa everything. She cried and told him he was an idiot. She was mad at him for about five minutes, but she couldn't stay that way, even though the feeling of betrayal and the pain of all those hurt and killed would take longer to go away. But the guilt would now be Matt's to carry. His actions had caused a lot of pain for a lot of people, and he would have to deal with them. They had been through too much together for her not to forgive him, plus, he had saved her life. She gave him a huge hug, saying, "You ever do something like that again and I'll shoot you myself!" But her tears took the bite out of her words.

Rissa finally got to go home, knowing everyone was going to be okay and knowing she was safe again. Thanksgiving was just around the corner, she had the store to take care of, Matt to take care of while he was recuperating, her relationship with Stone to consider, and a house she had to get in order—and she couldn't have been more eager to get started on everything. She was thinking how she appreciated everything so much more now. With her mind preoccupied, she was astounded when she walked into her home. She was surprised to see that her house was put back in order. Since she had been staying with Matt at the hospital she was wondering who had done this when there was a knock at her door. Even though in her head she knew she was safe, she hesitated. Then the phone rang, and she reached for it, never taking her eyes off the door.

"Hello?"

"Hey there."

"Stone! Where are you? I haven't seen you for days."

"I'm at your front door. Do you think you could open it for me?" Stone said with laughter in his voice.

Rissa hung up the phone, flung the door open, and flew into Stone's arms. Stone laughed. "I missed you too!"

"Where have you been?"

"Well, between getting loose ends tied up and dealing with the press, I've been trying to get some work done on a friend's house. Apparently a mad man and woman broke into her home and destroyed it. I figure after all she has been through, she didn't deserve to come home to a mess."

Tears welled up in her eyes as she looked at the man she loved. "That's the sweetest thing I've ever heard. I bet she appreciated you doing that for her."

"It wasn't just for her. If you'll notice there's a brand-new, *comfy* couch!"

Rissa laughed as she hugged Stone tighter.

"Ready for our first date?" Stone asked. Rissa couldn't think of anything she would rather do more.

"THAT'S ALL I CAN TAKE. I'm done!" Stone said after their third date, if you could call three days of not being separated "dates."

Rissa didn't understand. They had spent the most wonderful three days getting to know each other better than anyone else knew them.

"I can't take this. I don't want to date anymore. I know what I want and I think you do too."

Rissa smiled and for the first time in three days, felt tears welling up in her eyes.

"Rissa, I love you. I don't want to be away from you. I want to know I'll spend my life with you. I need you and I love you. Rissa, will you marry me?"

"Yes!" she said as she flung herself into the arms of the man she had waited her whole life for.

e|LIVE

listen|imagine|view|experience

AUDIO BOOK DOWNLOAD INCLUDED WITH THIS BOOK!

In your hands you hold a complete digital entertainment package. In addition to the paper version, you receive a free download of the audio version of this book. Simply use the code listed below when visiting our website. Once downloaded to your computer, you can listen to the book through your computer's speakers, burn it to an audio CD or save the file to your portable music device (such as Apple's popular iPod) and listen on the go!

How to get your free audio book digital download:

1. Visit www.tatepublishing.com and click on the e|LIVE logo on the home page.
2. Enter the following coupon code:
   ba01-b2ca-71f8-ecf8-767a-1f67-c02f-7def
3. Download the audio book from your e|LIVE digital locker and begin enjoying your new digital entertainment package today!